A CHRISTMAS ESCAPE

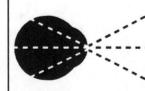

This Large Print Book carries the
Seal of Approval of N.A.V.H.

A CHRISTMAS ESCAPE

ANNE PERRY

THORNDIKE PRESS
A part of Gale, Cengage Learning

GALE
CENGAGE Learning·

Farmington Hills, Mich • San Francisco • New York • Waterville, Maine
Meriden, Conn • Mason, Ohio • Chicago

GALE
CENGAGE Learning®

LIBRARY OF CONGRESS CATALOGING-IN-PUBLICATION DATA

Perry, Anne.
    A Christmas escape / Anne Perry. — Large print edition.
      pages cm. — (Thorndike Press large print basic)
    ISBN 978-1-4104-8035-4 (hardback) — ISBN 1-4104-8035-6 (hardcover)
    1. Murder—Investigation—Fiction. 2. Large type books. 3. Christmas stories. I. Title.
    PR6066.E693C4655 2015b
    823'.914—dc23   2015035676

Published in 2015 by arrangement with Ballantine, an imprint of Random House, a division of Penguin Random House LLC

To those who believe
in starting again

Charles Latterly stared across the untroubled sea at the shore they were fast approaching. The mountain rose sharply, as symmetrical and uncomplicated as a child's drawing. The sky above was midwinter blue. At home in England they would be expecting snow at this time in December, but here, so close to Sicily, the wind off the salt water was mild. The small boat barely rocked.

He had been looking forward to

this break from the reality of London, work and the routine of his life, which lately had seemed more meaningless than ever. The recent death of his wife had given him an acute feeling of loss, but not in the way he had expected. There was no deep ache of bereavement. It forced him to realize that perhaps he had felt alone for a long time.

Would three weeks on Stromboli, a volcanic island in the Tyrrhenian, accomplish anything, change anything inside him? Would it heal the sense of helplessness, the bitterness of endless small failures? Maybe. It would certainly give him a long time to think, uninterrupted by the petty details of life.

He was in his midforties, yet he

felt old.

They were almost at the shore. He could see men on the wharfs busy unloading fishing boats. There were small houses along the front, and streets leading inland, climbing quite steeply. It all looked simple and homely, probably much as it had done for two thousand years or more.

The mountain was bigger than it had seemed at a distance. It towered above them, almost bare of vegetation except for patches of grass. The terrain looked smooth, even gentle from here.

It was time to pay attention to landing. The boat was only feet away from the wharf edge. Ropes were tossed and made fast. A man shouted in broken English for Charles to get out, to hold on so he didn't slip. They were all cheerful, smiling to make up for the words they didn't know.

Charles thanked the men in polite English, and accepted a steadying hand so as not to fall on the wet stones. He should make an effort to learn a little Italian. It would be a courtesy.

Someone passed him up his case. He had brought only the necessities: a minimum of clothes, a pair of boots, toiletries, and a couple of books. His intention was to spend his time walking as much as possible.

He knew that the hostelry where he was staying was quite remote and a long way from the port village — too far to walk with a case — so he hired a pony cart and driver to take him up the side of the mountain.

It was a pleasant ride, although the rough roads were quite steep in places. As they moved away from the water's edge, Charles realized that the landscape was actually far more varied than he had thought. The central cone of the volcano was not as symmetrical as it had seemed from below, at sea. It towered above them, bare toward the top, as if shorn of its grass and shrubs. Yet it had a kind of beauty that was brave but also almost barbaric.

His driver nodded. "She sleep

now," he said, showing gaps in his teeth as he smiled. "She wake up. You see."

Charles thought that he would rather not, but it would be impolite to say so. They were passing through rolling grassy country now. He imagined that in the spring and summer it would be full of flowers and butterflies, probably bees. A good place to walk.

They passed a few small settlements, some of whose narrow streets were cobbled, others, merely dry earth. The limestone houses were whitewashed. They looked as if they had been there forever. Women were busy with picking herbs or gathering in laundry. Children played, running and hiding, fighting with sticks for swords. Old men stood by a fountain on the street corner and stopped their conversation long enough to look briefly at the passersby.

As they drove, the driver gave commentary Charles did not understand, though he smiled and nodded at suitable intervals. He was relieved when they finally arrived at the low, rambling house well beyond the villages that was to be his home for the next three weeks.

"Thank you," he said as the man handed him his case. He paid the agreed amount and, as the pony and cart set off back toward the shore, he turned to look for his host.

The low midwinter sun cast a warm light on the stone house, slight shadows hiding blemishes and giving it an infinitely comforting look.

Then a man came out of the door and hurried toward him, a broad smile on his face, his hand held out.

"I am Stefano," he said cheerfully. "You must be Signor Latterly, yes? Good. Welcome to Stromboli. Is beautiful, yes?" He waved his arm in a broad sweep to include the huge, looming mountain and the arch of the sky, which was already darkening in the east. The fire of sunset in the west was painting the sea with color. A faint wind stirred, carrying the scent of the grasses.

"Yes, it is," Charles said quickly.

"I look forward to exploring."

"Tomorrow," Stefano agreed. "You have come a long way. Now you are tired. You eat. I have something for you. I show you your room. Yes? Come." Without waiting for Charles to reply, he led the way past the front of the house, along a small passage between buildings, and out into a courtyard with a bubbling fountain in it.

Charles had no time to look at it or admire the stone fish that formed its base. Stefano briskly led him into another open-air passage at the far side of the courtyard and opened the second door along.

"This is your room," he said with a flourish. "You are welcome. Kitchen is that way." He pointed.

"Come when you are ready. I make you something to eat, yes?" He patted his ample stomach. "Nobody sleep well empty. Not good. I look after you, you leave Stromboli a new man!" He smiled widely. "Yes?"

"Yes . . . yes, please," Charles accepted, walking past Stefano and inside. He set his case down, staring around him. The room was small, containing a bed, a table and chair, and a washstand. There was also one chest of drawers and a makeshift closet composed of several hooks behind a curtain. The floor was tiled in a warm earth shade. There was a bathroom through a small door, to be shared with his immediate neighbor. He did not care for that, but it was acceptable. It was all immaculately clean. The cool air through the open window smelled of dry earth.

He unpacked, changed his shirt for a fresh one, and washed the other. When he was ready, he left his room and walked along the passageway to the kitchen as Stefano had indicated.

Stefano looked up from the bench where he had been chopping a fine green herb. There was a piece of broiled fish on a plate on the bench beside him, garnished with bright red tomato.

"You are hungry?" Stefano said cheerfully. "Fish? A little vegetable? Bread? Yes?" He held out the plate and gestured toward a table with a chair pulled up to it. He took a carafe of red wine and poured two glasses full. "A little raw still," he said, putting one glass on the table in front of Charles and the other in the second place, where he sat down himself.

"Eat," he encouraged. "Give thanks to God, and enjoy." He reached across and took one of the slices of fresh crusty bread, dipped it in olive oil, and put it into his mouth.

Charles found himself doing the same. He must have been far hungrier than he realized. The food was delicious and he ate it all without giving it thought.

"You like to walk?" Stefano asked cheerfully.

"Yes, indeed," Charles agreed. "How far up can I go?"

"All the way up to the crater. But you have to be very careful. Never go up alone, in case you fall. Always take someone with you, and let me know."

"Is it dangerous?" Charles said with some surprise.

"It's rattling and making noise most of the time," Stefano answered. "Just take care. Don't go too close to the crater. It's always a good idea not to climb close. You hear me, signor? Don't worry, lava doesn't come this way. Just rocks now and again. We hide in cellar. Come out again."

"Yes," Charles agreed quietly. "Of course. I hadn't thought of going to the crater anyway."

Stefano's face split in a wide smile. "Of course not, not tonight, anyway. But it will call you. You'll go to it one day."

Charles stood up slowly. The meal had been excellent, and suddenly he was very tired. Nothing seemed as good as the idea of sleep.

He slept very well. The long train trip here had been pleasant from Paris to Milan, then south to Rome, and then Naples, and on south again. It had ended with the journey over the open water. But when he awoke to a small room full of sunlight, where everything was unfamiliar, it seemed less like an adventure. Now Charles simply felt a very long way from home, and hopelessly trapped. Stromboli was an island. No one came or went except by sea. Everyone here was a stranger speaking a language he did not understand.

He lay still, staring at the white ceiling. Then he turned over and looked at his watch sitting on the table beside the bed. It was half past nine!

He sat bolt upright, threw off the bedclothes, and stared around, remembering where everything was: the ewer of water, the bowl, the bathroom next door, the clothes he had hung on the hooks behind the curtain.

In fifteen minutes he was washed, shaved, and ready to look for breakfast. Now that he thought about it, he was actually very hungry.

He went out and started to walk in the direction he remembered from last night. Everything looked different, larger in the bright sunlight of the day. As soon as he passed the line of bedroom doors and crossed the paved yard with its softly bubbling fountain, he looked up and realized how large and how close the mountain was. Its enormous cone loomed up into the sky, paler than he expected. At first he thought it was covered by snow, then he realized it was ash.

"It's sort of beautiful, in an odd way, isn't it?" A girl's voice came to him from a few feet away.

He turned around quickly. He

had not been aware of anyone else there.

She smiled with a little shrug. It was a movement both gawky and graceful. She was tall and slim, and — he guessed — about fourteen years old. She had honey-brown hair, bleached lighter on top by the sun, almost gold. She was too young to have it pinned up. It was in a thick braid. Perhaps she was going to be a beauty, but all he noticed now was the dark blue of her eyes and her hopeful smile.

"Sorry," she said. "I didn't mean to startle you. You've just arrived, haven't you." It was a conclusion rather than a question.

"Yes . . ." Charles agreed.

"I'm Candace Finbar." She held

out her hand straight in front of her, just as if she were a boy.

He took it and felt her firm, cool grip. "I'm Charles Latterly," he responded. "I'm happy to meet you, Miss Finbar."

She raised her chin a little and looked at him with considerable dignity. "You may call me Candace." Then she laughed at herself.

"Thank you," he said perfectly seriously. "Since we are being informal, you had better call me Charles, or you will make me feel very old and I'm not in the mood for that."

"Do you like to climb? I do. It's a volcano, you know? It's not dead. It erupts quite often." Then she shook her head. "But there's no need to be afraid of it. At least that's what Uncle Roger says. It's been grumbling on for three thousand years, according to Stefano. But the villages are all still here." She looked around at the courtyard where they were, and the white walls of the surrounding house with its extra bedrooms and the sheds of various sorts. The walls were unblemished by fire or smoke.

She faced Charles again, smiling. "Even though we're closer to it than other villages, it's mostly just like a lot of old people: It complains and uses some harsh language, but it doesn't really do anything."

"Oh dear!" he said, with amusement now. "Is that your experience of old people? Sound and fury, and no substance?"

A faint blush colored her cheeks more deeply than the gold of sun- and windburn.

"No, that isn't fair," she said honestly. "It's only some. I get fed up with Mr. Bailey and Mr. Quinn making sideways remarks at each other that never really mean any- thing. We know them from back home in Buckinghamshire, but they've never behaved this badly before. If I acted like that, Uncle Roger would tell me to grow up and not be so silly. I think some- times that he'd like to tell them, but of course he can't."

"Mr. Bailey and Mr. Quinn stay- ing here?" Charles inquired.

Candace shrugged again. "Yes.

We've been here for about a few weeks now. Most of us are leaving after Christmas. You'll get to meet them. You won't really be able to avoid it. Colonel Bretherton's all right. He's a bit stuffy, and he never really knows what to say, but he's quite nice."

"Dear me. And Uncle Roger?" he added.

She realized he was teasing her and responded with spirit, as if she liked the acceptance it implied.

"Oh, he's fine. I like Uncle Roger. Which I suppose is a good thing. He's my guardian. My grandfather was his brother, but he died when he was a young man. Uncle Roger took care of my grandmama, his sister-in-law. I don't think he always approved of her, but he really loved her anyway." She said that with evident satisfaction and looked straight at him, waiting for his reply.

He wondered what had happened to her parents that she had a great-uncle as guardian at such a young age. Then he was surprised that it should even cross his mind, let alone matter to him. With her soft face and eager eyes and the beginning of such individual grace, she seemed to him very vulnerable; he wanted to think someone was not only duty bound to care for her but also well able to.

However, it was absolutely none of his concern, and it would be intrusive to ask.

"I'm glad Uncle Roger is not like

the mountain," he said as gravely as he could, hoping she would understand what he meant.

She giggled, and then stifled it immediately. "He is, a little bit," she replied. "Like it now, anyway."

He raised his eyebrows in question.

She accepted the invitation eagerly. Clearly she had been waiting for it.

"All old and living quietly in the sun, not making any fuss," she told him, watching his face to see how he took it.

He found an answer far more easily than he expected to. He was not in the least used to conversing with fourteen-year-old girls, especially not as if they were old friends.

"I think I should like him," he said honestly. "I'm glad he is here with you."

"So am I. He even walks up the hill sometimes." She looked beyond him at the great silent mountain. "There are some nice ways to go, lots of grasses and things. And you can see way over to the water. It gives you the feeling of being like one of the ancient goddesses, who could see all the world just by look-ing around them." A shadow crossed her face. "Mr. Bailey climbs right up to the crater," she said with a sniff. Plainly she did not like Mr. Bailey. "Stefano tells us not to; it's dangerous. The mountain is asleep, he says. It's not dead!"

Charles turned and looked up

into the shining silence.

"Do you think it would get offended," she asked him, "if we go up there and walk all over it, stand on the edge, and look down inside it? It seems sort of intrusive, don't you think?"

Charles turned back to look at her. She was perfectly serious. To her the mountain was an entity and deserved respect. A curious child.

"I hadn't thought of that," he replied. "It's a long way up. And according to what I've heard, it does erupt fairly often, and has as far back as records go."

Candace nodded, her expression showing that she was happy with his understanding. "The noises it makes sound to me like Mr. Bailey when he is asleep," she added, then giggled again.

"You think that's a good description, don't you?" he observed.

"Yes . . . I'm sorry. Is that rude of me? Please don't tell Uncle Roger I said so." She looked at him with a flicker of anxiety.

"I wouldn't dream of it," he promised. "I shall no doubt meet Mr. Bailey and form my own opinion of him. I might agree with you."

"And don't be too hard on Colonel Bretherton," she urged. "He's quite nice, if you give him a chance. He really likes Mrs. Bailey. I think he's sorry for her."

"Is something wrong with Mrs. Bailey?" Charles asked.

She rolled her eyes and gave him

a withering look. She did not bother to reply.

"I see," he said quietly. "And Mr. Quinn, what is he like?" He didn't really care, but he was amused to hear her opinion of everyone.

"Oh, he's a writer," she said without hesitation. "Everybody says he's terribly good."

"Everybody?"

"Well . . . except for Mr. Bailey," she said, biting her lip. "He keeps making remarks that could have different meanings. He says that the book is so terribly clever, it's as if Mr. Quinn had been there himself — only the way he says it, it sounds as though he doesn't mean it. That he means something else entirely."

"Well, maybe Mr. Quinn was there?" Charles suggested. "Couldn't he have been?"

She laughed. "Hardly! Actually the book he's famous for is wonderful. I wasn't supposed to read it because it's very grown-up. Uncle Roger says it's much too risqué for me. But I think it's marvelous."

Now Charles was really interested. How had this at once innocent and precocious child come across a copy of this apparently unsuitable book?

"So you've read it?" He feigned a degree of innocence himself.

She bit her lip. "You think I shouldn't have? I was told not to." She looked at him with a certain defiance, her dark blue eyes meeting his unblinkingly. Then she smiled and turned away. "It isn't really bad, you know. It's just . . . about a woman who cares very much about being alive. It's full of laughter."

"What is it called?" He knew he had not read it himself because he had not read anything purely for pleasure in years.

"Fire," Candace replied.

A memory came back to him of a conversation he had half listened to at some party or other. *"Fire,"* he repeated. "By Percival Quinn?"

"Yes, yes," she responded eagerly. "You do know it!"

"I know *of* it. It's quite famous, although very recent. Well, well! So we have Percival Quinn here. How interesting . . ."

She pursed her mouth. "Don't be too pleased. He's not nearly as interesting as the book. Honestly, I'm not being mean — he really isn't. That's more or less what Mr. Bailey keeps saying."

"Perhaps he's shy? Mr. Quinn, I mean."

She rolled her eyes again, gently this time, as if she were being very patient with someone a trifle slow-witted.

"They don't like each other, Charles." She tried out his name shyly, but with a touch of pleasure, as if she were being grown-up, equal for the first time. "What they say to each other is really all about themselves and how they feel. Our neighbor back home has children who do that. They're about eight!" She giggled again.

In spite of himself he smiled, almost laughed. "But it's a good book? Did you read enough of it to know what it's about?"

"Oh, yes! It's the story of an old lady. She's remembering all the wonderful things she did in her life. The people she loved and hated. All the admirers she had. You don't always know if she really did what she's describing, or if it's just that she wanted to — but it seems like she saw everything, tasted it all, and had such fun!" She looked up at the mountain, then back at Charles. "I'd like to be like her, always really alive, never taking anything for granted, never being ordinary. She'd have liked it here. She'd have liked that mountain. But she wouldn't have been satisfied unless it erupted, sent fire and boiling rocks all over the place. Not hurt anybody, of course. But . . . but made an exhibition of itself! Really . . . blew a hole in the sky!"

Charles liked her analogy. It was melodramatic but full of hope, excitement, and hunger for life. These were all the things he had stopped feeling a long time ago. An outrageous thought occurred to him.

"What do you suppose is on the other side of the sky?" he asked her, then instantly wished he had not. It was stupid, and would confuse her. She would think he was not taking her seriously, and — for all her imaginings — she was very serious, as only those at the beginning of life can be.

She stared at him. "What a wonderful thing to say!" she exclaimed. "You're not really old at all, are you!" Her smile was beautiful. "I never thought of that. The other side of the sky. One day I'll write a book and that is what I'll call it. I'll go around the world looking for the answer, like Lucy in Mr. Quinn's book. I'll never stop looking, just as she didn't. Do you think that if you spend all your life looking for answers, when you die then you find them?"

"It's as good a description of

heaven as any I've heard," he admitted. "Better than angels sitting on a cloud playing a harp, anyway."

"Oh, that would be terrible!" she exclaimed in horror. "I don't like harps all that much. Couldn't I have a trumpet? Or drums? I like drums."

This time he laughed outright, picturing her sitting on a cloud with a full set of kettledrums, and all the other angels with their hands over their ears.

"You think I'm silly . . ." She was uncertain of herself now, watching for his reaction.

"Not at all," he denied. "If you are good enough to get to heaven, then you should be able to play any kind of music you want to. Your cloud sounds like a lot more fun than one with only harps. Aren't you hungry?"

"No. I had breakfast an hour ago. Didn't you? Oh! Of course not. You've just got up. I'm sorry. Now it's too late." She looked crestfallen. "But I'll take you to the kitchen. I'm sure Stefano will get you something really good. He makes the best bread in the world."

"I think I would like the best bread in the world," Charles accepted. "In fact I would accept even the second best."

She turned and gave him a hard, sober stare. "He doesn't have that," she said, then burst into laughter.

Charles did indeed have an excellent breakfast of fresh crusty bread, slightly salty butter, and thick dollops of homemade apricot jam. Stefano watched him eat it with almost as much relish as Charles actually eating it.

When he had finished, he stayed to watch Stefano preparing luncheon. Stefano took his choice of tomatoes, some fresh green leaves, and other vegetables Charles was not familiar with. As he watched the Italian consider each leaf, each herb, before accepting or rejecting it, he began to appreciate how much Stefano enjoyed creating dishes that would dazzle all the senses. The meal was designed to please the eye with its riot of color: reds and greens, yellows, oranges, and pale greeny-white. There was a variety of shapes and textures. Every so often Stefano would pop something into his mouth to make sure the taste was the best he could find.

"There!" he said eventually, looking at Charles and beaming with satisfaction. "They will like, yes?"

"It's beautiful," Charles said honestly. "I hope we deserve it."

Stefano shrugged his plump shoulders. "Not matter," he said happily. "Is good. Is enough. Not taste it properly is a shame, but their shame, not mine. I try something else next time, maybe." He laughed. "Maybe not. Is good for you. Vegetable is also good for you." He moved over to a wide porcelain tub with a wooden lid. From inside he took some very large, already cooked prawns. "You like?" he asked Charles.

"Oh, yes," Charles agreed heartily. "Of course I like."

Stefano took one, cracked it to remove the inner flesh, and offered it to Charles. "You tell me, is good enough for our guests?"

Charles ate it enthusiastically. "Oh, very definitely," he said with a smile. "Are they good enough for these? If not, then we had better keep them for us."

"You are a bad man, signor," Stefano said happily. "You tempt me. Perhaps we should try another, yes? Just to make sure . . ."

At luncheon, Charles was introduced to the rest of the guests at
the house.

Candace came into the dining
room looking demure and very well
behaved. She glanced at him once,
almost shyly, and then looked away.
She was accompanied by an elderly
man, who was tall, thin, and white-
haired. He had a mild face, which
was ascetic and a little pale except
for the beginning of sunburn on his
nose and high cheekbones.

"Roger Finbar," he introduced
himself. "You must be Latterly.
How do you do? This is my great-
niece, Candace Finbar."

"How do you do, sir?" Charles
replied. Then he glanced at Candace as if he had not seen her

before, and saw the relief brilliant in her eyes for an instant, then gone again. "Miss Finbar," he acknowledged her.

The only other woman in the party was decidedly handsome, but in a calm and gentle way that did not especially appeal to Charles. She could not have been the heroine of a book anyone would have entitled *Fire.* She was introduced by Finbar as Mrs. Isla Bailey.

"Where is your husband?" Finbar asked to fill the momentary silence when the polite acknowledgments had been made.

"Not returned yet from his walk," Mrs. Bailey replied. "He must have gone farther than he intended. Please don't wait for him."

"Certainly not," another man agreed, coming into the room from the opposite door. He was of at least average height with fair hair and dull, precise features. He was very casually dressed, but Charles could tell at a glance that his clothes were of excellent quality and perfectly tailored to his slightly lopsided physique.

He gave a faint bow, more just a gesture of his head.

"Percival Quinn," he murmured. "I presume you are Latterly, the final member of our group?"

"Yes, Mr. Quinn. How do you do, sir?" Charles acknowledged him. He regarded Quinn with interest. So this was the man who had written the book about the woman who had filled her life with such passion. Charles was inclined to agree with Candace; Quinn did not look like a man whose imagination could create such a work. Perhaps this went to show that it was one of life's classic mistakes to judge the heart or mind of a person by the cast of their features!

Just as everyone had chosen a place at the single long table, they were joined by another man. There was no hesitation in Charles's mind as to his identity. He was tall, very straight-backed and square-shouldered. His upper lip was decorated with a meticulously trimmed mustache and his cheeks were of rich color from the sun- and windburn of many seasons.

This had to be Colonel Bretherton.

"Late," Bretherton said unhappily. "I apologize. Mrs. Bailey, Miss Finbar." He looked at Charles as he pulled out his chair with a slight squeak as its legs scraped the floor. "Bretherton. You must be Latterly. How do you do, sir?"

Stefano bustled in with steaming pasta to add to the vegetables and the huge dish of prawns. He beamed at his guests, bade them welcome, and told them to enjoy. There were glasses on the table, and a carafe of wine from which they were to help themselves.

There was only one chair unoccupied.

Into this pleasant gathering the last member arrived late. He was a middle-aged man, vigorous and wiry. His brown hair was receding slightly, making his broad brow even more prominent. Now he looked irritated.

"I see you have begun without me." It sounded very much like a criticism as he pulled his chair out, banging it against the wall behind him deliberately. "I'm glad I didn't keep you waiting." His tone did not convey pleasure. He helped himself from the various bowls and began eating immediately. He had had several mouthfuls before he spoke again. He looked first at Isla Bailey, who said nothing, then across at Charles.

"Since no one is going to introduce me, I suppose I had better introduce myself. I am Walker-Bailey. I assume someone has introduced you to my wife, Isla? Bretherton, no doubt." He shot a hard glance at the colonel but did not leave him time to deny it.

"Charles Latterly," Charles responded. "How do you do, Mr. Bailey?"

"Walker-Bailey," Bailey corrected him. "Not exactly the place to pass over one's card, but it is hyphenated."

Charles knew that he was supposed to apologize for the slip, but the man's disregard for the courtesies of the meal annoyed him, so he didn't. The ease had gone from the room.

Bailey turned to Quinn. "Been

writing again this morning?" he asked. "Seeking the muse?"

"If you want to put it that way," Quinn replied, taking another mouthful of salad.

Bailey smiled, but the curve of his lips was not kind. "It must be terribly difficult to find such a . . ." he hesitated, looking for exactly the right word, ". . . unique, passionate voice," he finished.

Isla looked uncomfortable, glancing at her husband, then at Quinn.

Bretherton cleared his throat but ended up saying nothing.

"Did you imagine writing was easy?" There was a note of challenge in Quinn's voice, but solely for Bailey. He ignored everyone else.

Bailey swallowed his mouthful of food and took a sip of wine. "Perhaps you made an error — a technical one, of course, not a literary one — in letting Lucy die at the end of your . . . novel?" he suggested, looking again at Quinn.

"Oh, no!" Candace interrupted with certainty in her whole bearing. "It was right. It was the end of her life. Anything more after that would have ruined it."

Everyone at the table turned to look at her, with varying expressions of surprise or disbelief, except Charles, who already knew that she had read it. Finbar, who should have known better, seemed the most taken aback.

Bailey raised his eyebrows very

high. "I beg your pardon?"

Candace blushed, but she met his eyes without flinching and repeated exactly what she had said.

"I heard you," Bailey said tartly. "I was giving you an opportunity to rephrase your remarks a little more appropriately."

Charles spoke before he considered the wisdom of it. "They seemed perfectly appropriate to me. If a story is complete, then you diminish it by adding more." He remembered some advice from years ago. "The recipe for a perfect speech is to begin at the beginning, go through the middle, come to the end, and then for heaven's sake stop!"

"Most amusing," Bailey said

dryly. "Who did you say you were again? I apologize, but I don't recall."

"Charles Latterly, Mr. Bailey," Charles said deliberately.

"He likes to be known as Walker-Bailey," Colonel Bretherton added, with a discreet but very genuine smile.

Candace smothered a giggle in her napkin. Then, aware that everyone was looking at her, she turned it into a sneeze, and then a second one.

Charles passed her a glass of water, not with the idea that it would be any use at all, but just as a sign of solidarity.

Finbar sighed, but shot him a look of appreciation.

Bailey peered at her, then turned to her great-uncle. "I'm surprised you allow a child her age to read such things. It has some rather . . . explicit passages in it, don't you think? All imagination, of course. I cannot conceive of the notion that Quinn actually asked elderly ladies how they felt about such . . . physical . . . behavior . . ." He stopped, clearly uncertain how to say what he meant without being crude in front of his wife and Candace.

Quinn started to say something, then stopped, possibly for the same reason.

Candace looked down and reached for the glass of water again, to hide her expression.

"I didn't allow it," Finbar said

with grace. "I was not aware she had read it. But she is very nearly old enough to know about such things. I thought the descriptions were rather good, actually. Emotional, tender, rather than simply graphic."

"I can't imagine how you come to be guardian of a child, and a girl," Bailey said gravely. "What on earth were her parents thinking of?"

"Please . . ." Isla implored, her voice thick with embarrassment and distress, both for Candace and for Finbar.

"Probably that they would not die so young!" Charles filled the silence.

Finbar looked across at Isla, a gentle pity in his eyes. "Looking after Candace is a privilege I inherited largely by default."

Bretherton turned slightly in his chair and stared at Bailey.

"Did you walk up toward the crater this afternoon?" he inquired with a tone of interest he could not have felt.

Bailey stared at him for a moment, startled out of his contemplation of Quinn's book and Candace's guardian.

"Did you?" Isla echoed.

"Of course I did," Bailey replied. "It was well worth the climb. The views are unlike anything else in the world. The sky, the sea, and fire on the earth right under your feet. There is a sense of timelessness one cannot even imagine anywhere else.

No wonder the ancients believed in gods the way we only pretend to now. They felt the enormity of creation! We only sit in polite rows in man-made churches and talk about sets of rules. I recommend that each of you climb as far as you can, and look at the marvels of the world."

No one answered him. Perhaps they felt no need.

Before the silence could gather weight, Stefano came in from the kitchen with a large bowl of fruit: late autumn apples, and a few odd-shaped fruits that Charles had not seen before.

"You should finish with something sweet," Stefano said, setting the bowl down. "Maybe you come back one year when the peaches are ripe? Such peaches we have, the juice runs down your chin!"

"Thank you." Isla smiled at him. "It seems everything here is so good."

"But of course!" He beamed at her. "You think I serve to you anything that is not the best? Never!"

Bailey opened his mouth, but at a glare from both Quinn and Charles, he closed it without speaking.

Stefano smiled at them all and went out again to the kitchen. Charles realized he had his own way of dealing with ungraciousness, without ever descending to rudeness. He found himself not only liking the man but admiring him. It was a good feeling: warmer and easier than anything he could remember in a long time — too long to bring back to mind with any clarity. He knew that, and acknowledged it as probably no more than the unfamiliarity of the place, Stefano's good humor, and of course the warm, cloudless sky.

After lunch was over Charles walked alone around the area immediately next to the house. The meticulous care with which it was tended pleased him. Whitewash over all the stones and clay of the buildings was a very simple decoration, but it was also clean and fresh. Nothing was ornate, but the doors and windows were functional and that quality had its own beauty.

He was strolling toward one of the more private areas of the garden, just outside the larger rooms, when he heard voices within. He recognized them straightaway. One of them was that of Isla Bailey.

He stopped, not wanting to intrude.

"I've already told you! I don't want to go." The reply came from Bailey, as Charles would have expected. "You're making a fuss over nothing." His tone was abrupt, more than irritated.

"It may be nothing to you!" she responded. Now her voice was thick with emotion. Clearly she was distressed. "I care very much. I don't know why you can't see that!"

"I can't see it because it is all in your own feelings . . ."

"We're talking about feelings!" she protested.

"*You* are. I am talking about facts," he corrected her tartly. "We need to be realistic."

"There's nothing unrealistic about staying."

They may have had the argument many times before — from the distress and exasperation in their voices that would be easy to believe — yet apparently there was deep disagreement between them still.

"It's far too big." He made an exaggeratedly patient attempt to explain his point to her.

Charles could not help imagining

the sneer in his face.

"We do not need two acres of garden and an orchard, Isla," Bailey continued. "The outbuildings are totally useless to us and will cost a fortune to reroof."

"We can do it bit by bit . . ."

"For what? We don't need an apple house. Be reasonable. The orchard is gone! At least you agreed we had to sell that!"

She seemed to choke on her words. "I know that! But why tear down a perfectly good storehouse just because we don't have the apples?"

"We're not going to tear it down." Now his patience was clearly exhausted and it was as if he were speaking to someone mentally simple. "We are going to sell it, Isla. Whoever buys it can do as they wish. It is not our concern."

She was close to weeping. The unshed tears were thick in her voice.

"It's my house, Walker. My parents and grandparents are buried in the local chapel. I was born there. My . . . my only baby is buried there. You can't sell it!" The sob broke through all the barriers of her attempt at restraint.

Charles felt a deep, painful ache of pity for her. There was nothing whatever he could do to help. If she had inherited the property of which they were speaking, then at her marriage it automatically would have become her husband's. The law would say Bailey could do with it what he pleased. No act of law since then could change it back retroactively.

He stood frozen to the spot. There was gravel under his feet. If he moved, it would rattle and he would be heard.

"Isla," Bailey said more calmly, "pull yourself together. We have already agreed on it. We must move to a smaller place, preferably one nearer London . . ."

"It would cost more," she protested.

"It's not to save money!" The exasperation was audible in his tone, and in the little sigh as he drew in his breath. "We have plenty of money. It's just too big, too old, and too far out of the way."

"My friends are there!" she pleaded.

"You have friends all over the place. You'll make more. You always do. God knows why, with some of them. What on earth makes you defend a pompous, self-important fraud like Quinn?"

"You don't know he's a fraud!" she said angrily. "You just hate him because he wrote a brilliant book and everyone admires him for it."

"Of course he's a fraud." Now the deep derision was unmistakable and ugly. "He no more understands the passions and the laughter, the hunger for life in that character of his than . . . than bloody Bretherton does!"

Isla was silent.

Charles strained his ears unabashedly eavesdropping, but he could hear nothing.

Then there was a sharp slam of a door and the sound of Isla weeping quietly.

Charles wished there were something — anything — he could do to comfort her. But what was there to say? That he had overheard the whole conversation, and her husband was a brute? No one could stop the man from selling her home, even if she didn't want to. He wondered why Bailey didn't seem affected by the fact that their child was buried there. Presumably it had been his child also, but he had not carried it, given birth to it, or nursed it as she had. Perhaps the loss meant little to him. Or was that why he wanted to leave, no matter what it did to her?

Charles doubted that. Had Bailey felt any kind of grief, surely he would have been gentler with her.

And what was at the root of his loathing of Quinn? Just jealousy of a man who had spectacularly succeeded?

Charles could not help. The only service he could offer would be to keep secret that he had heard anything.

When could he move without rattling stones and letting her know there had been someone there? Not knowing who it was might be even worse for her.

He heard footsteps approaching from the other way: a heavy tread. The next moment there was a voice: certainly not Bailey returning. It was a moment before he recognized it was Bretherton's.

"I'm so sorry," Isla said clearly. "Dust in my eyes." She made a mighty effort to compose herself and sound normal.

"I suppose it's partly ash," Bretherton replied. "There must be centuries' worth of it around here."

"Yes, of course," she agreed. "I keep thinking that one day I'll walk up there and look. It's quite a long way."

"You mustn't go alone," he warned her gently. "If you slipped and hurt yourself, it could be ages before anyone found you. Please promise that you won't do that!"

She gave a rough little laugh, as if it hurt. "I promise you, Colonel, I won't. Maybe I'll go up one day when Mr. Finbar does."

"That would be a good idea." He did not offer to take her himself.

Charles wondered how long they had known each other. Was it before this trip to Stromboli? She called him "colonel" even in what they assumed to be complete privacy. There was a shyness in her voice but a warmth also. She liked Bretherton. Or perhaps she simply liked anyone who spoke to her kindly.

There were a few moments of silence; then Bretherton spoke

again.

"Are you sure there is nothing I can do to help?"

She took a deep breath. "There's nothing anyone can do," she said softly. "But thank you for asking. It . . . it's kind of you."

As Bretherton started to move, Charles left as quietly as he could, hoping his footsteps were masked by the sound of the other man's.

Back in his room, he collected a light jacket and put on his stronger boots, suitable for climbing on the harsh ash and boulder-strewn paths up toward the summit of the mountain.

He enjoyed stretching his legs and walking in the open. For the first half mile or so the path climbed only very slightly; then he felt it in the back of his legs as it became steeper. He was surrounded by tall, dry grasses of many sorts, grown from seeds long ripened and blown away by the wind. There were no flowers — it was far too late in the year — but he could see the husks of old seed heads, shells of where there had been flowers. There were also, in places, low scrub bushes that might well be green in the spring but were now dry and only faintly aromatic.

He stopped for a few moments, giving himself a rest, and time to turn slowly and look at the view. To one side of him the cone of Stromboli rose into the unbroken blue of the sky, almost symmetrical, at least from this point. It would be a stiff climb, but perhaps another day he would do it. It would be good for him to pit himself against it.

But what if he failed? What if a miserable creature like Bailey could do it, and he couldn't?

Why should that bother him? Wasn't he used enough to failure to take it in his stride? He ought to be. What had he ever succeeded at? His elder brother had died a hero in the Crimea. His sister was possibly even braver; she had gone out there as a nurse, voluntarily. No one had made her go. In fact, several people had tried to stop her. Not that trying to stop Hester had ever gained anyone a victory.

She had fulfilled her dreams, even

magnified them. And no one had arranged a suitable marriage for her! The idea made him smile, perhaps a little ruefully. She had married the man she loved — a highly unsuitable man he had seemed at the time — but she was truly happy.

Charles had stayed at home and done what he could to help his parents, without any success at all. That was almost too painful even to think of, and yet he did, even knowing how it would hurt.

It had been one of those wretched tricks guileless men believe, a plea by a returned soldier asking for help for his business. He had invoked Charles's elder brother's name and told some story of being with him the day before the battle in which he died. Charles should have paid more attention. And if he had been the sort of man his father had confidence in, his father would have asked Charles's opinion; he would have seen the lie for what it was — or at least not believed it so readily — and the whole terrible business might not have happened. There would have been no loss, no suicide, no shame and grief for his mother. She would still be alive.

Why had he never found the right words to give her heart to live? Hester would have. James would have, were he not dead and buried a thousand miles away. Charles had said and done everything he could think of — but it was not enough.

To be fair, Hester had never blamed him — she blamed herself for being too far away to help. But that did not alter the facts, nor his deep ache of failure.

He had married suitably. It had gone as well as most marriages, except that there had been no children. They had been loyal to each other, adequate companions. They seldom quarreled.

And yet he could never remember laughing.

Perhaps that summed it all up — no remembered laughter.

Now she was gone, and he was halfway up a volcano in the Tyrrhenian, wondering how to find some hunger for life, some passion, some belief in himself that would drive him with the kind of inner fire that Candace Finbar had read about in Quinn's book.

He started to walk upward again. It didn't truly matter if he reached the top or not, whether he could stand up there on what would seem like the roof of the world and stare downward into the crater of a live volcano where the molten rock of the earth was red-hot, like a beating heart of all life. But it would be a kind of victory, all the same.

There seemed to be some kind of path, at least a track where the grasses were flattened by human footsteps. He followed it automatically, perhaps because it was easier or maybe because it suggested that there might be someone else up there ahead of him.

It was another hard fifteen minutes before he saw them: two figures on the slope a hundred yards away, silhouettes against the vivid blue of the sky. He knew who they were instantly. One was a man, tall and a little bent as if he were weary. The other was as slender as a wand, head high, a coltish grace to her movement. They could only be Roger Finbar and Candace.

For a moment Charles was not sure if he wanted to catch up with them or not. His legs were tired and he was a little short of breath. Nevertheless, he started forward and increased his pace. He did not want it to seem as if the climb was too much for him.

He was panting a little, and fifty yards behind them, when Candace turned and saw him.

She called out to him, but the increasingly strong wind carried her words away. Then realizing that he had not heard her, she touched Finbar on the arm; he turned to look back, saw Charles, and waved. They stood still. Charles made an effort that tore at the back of his calves and set his lungs aching, but he caught up with them in moments. Then he had to give in and stop to catch his breath. They were very high up. The view was marvelous, as far and wide as the sea on all sides except where the volcano towered into the sky, a huge and brooding presence, almost naked of trees or growth at this altitude.

Candace was beaming.

"I thought you'd have to come. It's different, isn't it? I mean, it's not like anywhere else at all. Except I suppose other really big volcanoes. Have you ever been up Vesuvius? That's huge. It wiped out whole towns when it blew up in the time of Pliny the Younger, you know?"

Charles struggled to get his breath and speak in a voice something like normal.

"Yes," he agreed. "It's far bigger than this, and quiet nearly all the time. When it does blow, it's stupendous. Here there are spits and crackles a lot of the time."

She grinned at him. "I told you

that this morning."

Finbar touched her arm. "Candace, why don't you go on ahead of us a little way?"

She understood the hint at once. Nodding cheerfully, she walked off ahead of them.

Finbar sighed. "I'm afraid it is a little too far for me," he said as if it were an apology. "She has so much energy."

Charles sympathized with him. He watched as she went in an easy stride up the steeper incline, looking eagerly at the path on toward the caldera.

"We all did at that age," he replied.

"She shouldn't go up much farther alone." Finbar shook his head.

Charles looked at Finbar's face, pale beneath the sunburn, and said the only thing he could.

"I'll go with her, sir. Are you all right to return alone? It's quite a long way . . ."

Finbar smiled. "I'll take it slowly. Please tell her not to worry. I know she's young, and a trifle outspoken at times, but she has a gentle heart."

"I won't worry her unnecessarily, I promise," he answered.

"Thank you, sir," Finbar said seriously, his blue eyes very clear, his gaze direct. Then he turned and began the long walk back down to the level, and the white house now long out of sight.

Charles had to lengthen his stride

considerably to catch up with Candace. They were far up the mountainside now. The air was thinner, and there was a faint sharpness to it with an odor that might have been disagreeable to some, but Charles found it rather interesting.

When he caught up with her, she was staring into the distance and the blue glimmer of the sea far away and below them. There was no sound but the faintest breeze, and — this far up — very little vegetation and no apparent animal or even insect life. The ground beneath them was mostly ash.

Anxiety flickered across her face. "Where's Uncle Roger?"

"His legs were a little tired," Charles replied, trying not to sound breathless. "He hoped you wouldn't mind if he went back. I promised I would see that you got down again safely."

"But he's all right?" she pressed.

"Yes. It's just a long way." Perhaps he shouldn't have concealed his lack of breath. "And getting steeper as we go up. I daresay the air's a little thinner, too."

She regarded him more closely. "Are you all right?"

Good heavens! Did she put him in the same bracket of age and corresponding frailty as Roger Finbar?

"Or are you trying to make me feel all right about Uncle Roger?" she went on.

To say she was frank would be an understatement.

"The latter," Charles replied a little tartly. "He would be very unhappy with me if I allowed you to be worried."

She looked taken aback, for once uncertain how to accept the remark. He noticed it with some satisfaction. In fact, he smiled back at her, meeting her eyes with something of a challenge.

She understood immediately. "All right. Let's go on up."

They climbed in silence for quite a distance, Candace always a few steps ahead of him. He appreciated that. It allowed him to see her all the time and know that while she was pushing herself, she was well within her strength. It also meant that if he was weary and had to grit his teeth to force himself on now and then, she did not know it. He realized now that he had been far too sedentary, not getting nearly enough exercise. It was not good for him. He was soft, weak where he should be strong. If this break over Christmas did nothing else for him, it would at least make him take more care of his health.

The next time they stopped, his legs were aching, and he was glad to see that Candace also seemed a little out of breath. Her cheeks were flushed, and she was drawing in lungsful of the thin, slightly acrid air, but she was smiling broadly, not just with victory but with the pure joy of adventure.

He looked around. They were

standing on rock and cinder now and there was no vegetation at all. Underfoot was all dust and solidified lava, and it was warm to the touch.

Was that a slight tremor, or did he imagine it?

"This is far enough," he said firmly.

"It's all right," she said with a meekness he had not expected. "I can feel it."

"A shake?" he asked with surprise. "I wasn't certain if I had imagined it."

"Not really a shake." She shook her head. "But it's uneasy, isn't it — as if it's asleep but having bad dreams?"

He could not have put it better.

"You speak as if it were alive." He said it lightly, as if it amused him, but her word "uneasy" was exactly the one he would have used. Ridiculous, really. It was rock!

"Can't you feel it?" She turned to look at him. "Through your feet! It is alive. It's the earth, the heart of it. We see only the skin on the very outside — like a fungus!"

"Delightful," he said sarcastically. "I hadn't thought of myself as a skin disease."

"Of course *you* hadn't . . . you're not a volcano." She smiled at him as if that were a perfectly reasonable point of view.

He took a step toward her, just in case she defied him and decided to go closer to the edge, perhaps even to look down into the burning heart of the mountain. Was it red? he wondered. Was it molten rock down far below them, seething and boiling where they could actually see it?

He was seized with a desire to know. How amazing to have stood this close to such a thing and never to know for certain. Perhaps he could see the naked heart of the earth, not covered over with a mantle of rock.

Candace was staring at him. Was she imagining the same thing?

"We should go back," Charles said, although he realized he was saying it more to himself than to her.

The fine dust at her feet slithered

a little and she almost lost her balance. She regained it quickly, holding out one arm to adjust her weight. Then she looked across at him. In that moment each knew that the other had thought of creeping over to the edge and looking down, wondering what they might see.

There was a puff of sharp-smelling wind. Another patch of lava dust slithered out of position and trickled down the mountain.

Candace swallowed hard.

A plume of either smoke or steam belched out of the caldera and drifted up into the sky, losing shape only as the wind slowly dispersed it.

"We're going down again,"

Charles announced. "Come on!"

Candace faced the crater. "You are having nightmares, old man," she said loudly and clearly. "Think of something nice, and go back to sleep." Then she turned back to Charles and began to walk down toward the vestiges of a path countless feet had made.

Charles kept up with her. The view ahead spread out as far as the sea, which was now shining like a polished jewel in the far distance. There was no one else in sight, no birds circling, no small creatures on the rock, which was gray-red in color but of the texture of a motionless sea. It was like a riptide stayed in a single instant.

Neither of them spoke until they

reached the first grass. Charles was amazed how beautiful he found it. No cultured plant in a garden had ever looked more passionately alive than these rough greenish-brown grasses springing out of the earth, finding roots and nourishment in what looked like a lifeless waste. What absurd courage!

He found himself smiling for no sensible reason. He was tired, his back ached, and his feet hurt. They were still miles from home. On the other hand, the weather was fine and dry, and the route was gently downhill the rest of the way. And no doubt Stefano would have made something delicious for dinner.

"Wasn't Mr. Walker-Bailey a beast at lunch?" Candace said suddenly, as if they had been discussing it only a few moments before.

"About Quinn's work? Yes," Charles agreed. "I admit, it had the effect of making me want to read it."

She laughed. "I'm glad. That's the last thing he would want. Although I don't know whether you would like it or not. You might be scandalized." She glanced sideways at him to see his reaction.

"Were you?" he returned.

"Oh, no." She sounded very grown-up, and looked so terribly young.

He thought immediately that she had been just a little upset by it, but she would never admit it. She was on the brink of adulthood; it lay ahead of her, whether she was ready for it or not. And from the tiny bit he knew of her, he was quite sure she would embrace it. She would never retreat from life, even when it might be wiser to do so.

"Then I think I might manage it," he said conversationally. "If I can't, then it will do me good to be scandalized."

She considered that in silence for several steps.

"Why do you think it would upset me?" He was too curious to let it go.

She weighed her answer while they walked another fifty yards or so. The track through the grasses was quite clear now, but there were still a few steep bits that required concentration.

"It's the way men think about women," she said at last. "I mean, if men fall in love with women, they sort of . . ." She very deliberately did not look at him. She seemed to be watching her step in the grasses, but he knew she was avoiding his eyes.

He waited for her to continue. He was interested in what she was going to say, but on the other hand, he did not want to embarrass her.

"They expect them to be all very pure and obedient," she went on in a rush. "We're not supposed to be told about anything . . . scandalous. It isn't ladylike. Women who enjoy that kind of thing are bad.

Actually I think I would rather be bad." There was a flush of color on the side of her face that he could see.

He was very careful not to smile. At this moment she looked so very young. He could easily understand the weight of Finbar's responsibility.

She walked for several more paces before she turned to face him.

"Have you any daughters?" she asked.

It was the last comment he had expected.

"No. No, I'm sorry to say, I haven't." He *was* sorry. Right at this moment he would like to have had a daughter more than anything else he could think of: a bright, funny, sensitive, impossibly brave daughter.

"Oh. I'm sorry." She was instantly contrite. "Maybe I shouldn't have asked. Uncle Roger says I ask all sorts of things I shouldn't. I just thought you might, because you seem to understand me. We can be friends, though, can't we? So I can still ask you things?"

"Of course we can," Charles agreed. His throat was choked with emotion. He was being absurd! He had never thought much about children before, and when he had, he had pictured sons. Now, in the space of a day, he felt as if he had been bereaved of an important pleasure.

She smiled at him, shy and

pleased. Then suddenly she increased her pace, and the next time
she spoke it was about old, ordinary
subjects.

"Mr. Walker-Bailey says that
Quinn is really a poor writer, which
is just stupid, because everyone
says the book is a masterpiece. He
also says that Quinn will never
write another one. What do you
think?"

"I think I need to read it," Charles
replied quite seriously. "I admit,
from what you say of the book, and
the heroine of it, Lucy . . . ?"

"Yes, Lucy. Nobody ever says
what her other name is."

"Right, Lucy . . . she doesn't
sound like the sort of woman whom
Quinn would understand at all,

never mind create. Which goes to show that we have no idea what people are like inside."

She smiled at him again. "Of course we don't. That's marvelous, don't you think? You could have all sorts of passionate dreams, wounds inside and no one else can see them, unless you allow them to." Her face clouded again. "But of course lots of people don't want to see. They don't care. I care! Don't you?"

That was a hard question to answer. The truth was that until now he had not cared greatly. Maybe that was part of his unhappiness. But he could not say that to her.

"The older I get, the more I care," he said. And that was definitely honest. Yesterday he had not cared enough. Today, as far as she was concerned, and perhaps Finbar, and Isla Bailey, even Bretherton, yes, he cared. Bailey's cruelty angered him. Charles didn't know them at all, but he wanted Isla to be able to keep her home. He felt for Bretherton's hopeless affection for her.

"But you're not so very old," she pointed out. "So maybe you are going to care a lot more yet?" She said it as if to comfort him, as if it were a happy new thought.

He was a great deal less sure about that, but he did not argue. They walked the rest of the way mostly in companionable silence, with just the occasional observation about a plant or the ever-changing view. Twice more, they noticed a plume of smoke or steam rise from the mountain and cast a momentary shadow across the land.

Sunset was a glory of hot color staining the sky across the west. They stood side by side watching it, both knowing that the darkness would come swiftly after, and they would have trouble picking their way over the uneven ground. It did not matter. Charles said nothing. He was certain in his own mind that Candace felt exactly as he did. This particular sunset would never happen again. There would not be exactly this banner of fire across the sky, quite such a delicate breath of turquoise above the cloud, like some ancient enamel, green, tender with age. The last colors would come in the same places, but perhaps the indigo of night would be somehow different.

When they moved on Candace turned to look at him once. He was certain she was smiling, but he could no longer see her face.

Dinner was excellent. Stefano had spent a good deal of the afternoon preparing baked fish for them, and arranged it with artistry on a large platter. It was decorated with winter vegetables, including potatoes baked and crisped so the edges were a delicate golden brown.

They were all gathered, except

Walker-Bailey.

Everyone was uncomfortable.

"Where the devil is the man?" Bretherton said under his breath to Charles. He looked at Isla, who had taken some care with her appearance, especially her hair, which was curled and dressed up on her head. She was wearing a soft muslin dress in a shade of pastel blue that was most flattering to her particular kind of beauty. His admiration was too plain for Charles to miss.

"I've no idea," Charles confessed. "I went up the mountain and I saw no sign of him there."

"One is tempted to hope that the damn fool fell into the sea," Bretherton said bitterly. "But unless he were washed up on the shore, we would never know." He colored a little uncomfortably at his own outspokenness. It was tactless, although possibly no one would be surprised.

Quinn was also less than composed about it. He clearly saw no reason why he should not express his annoyance.

"For heaven's sake, what is the matter with the man?" he demanded of no one in particular. "Even if he forgot his watch, the sunset is plain enough! Any fool can tell roughly how long it is until sundown. He knows what time we eat!"

"I think we should ignore it," Finbar said wearily. He looked tired, and Charles felt a pang of concern for him. He was the oldest person here by several years. The fact that he walked considerable distances did not mean he felt no exhaustion, or that he did not require a certain degree of regularity in mealtimes.

Candace was also dressed in a pale muslin, but of a much less sophisticated cut than Isla's. She looked curiously at Finbar, then at Charles, but it was Isla she spoke to.

"Mrs. Bailey, I don't wish to be discourteous, but would you mind if we begin to eat while Stefano's food is fresh and looking so delicious? I think it is a way of thanking him that he would appreciate. He goes to a lot of care to make our food exceptional."

Isla seemed to be relieved. "Yes, of course we should," she agreed. "I'm sorry that my husband is late. It is most inconsiderate of him, but he seems to lose track of time. I do apologize, and I would feel far better about it if we all began to eat."

"You have no need to apologize," Bretherton said quickly. "Nobody imagines it was within your control. But . . . thank you for making us feel at ease." He did not look at her, as if he had meant to say something different and at the last moment changed his mind.

Finbar sat at his usual place, and one by one everybody else took theirs, leaving one conspicuously empty seat for Walker-Bailey.

Stefano came in, beaming with satisfaction, and offered them a choice of white wines with their fish.

"And today I have a surprise for you," he said happily. "The fish is very light. I think perhaps you would like a dessert, yes? I have a special dish here for you. A delicate pastry, with fruit and thick cream. You will like . . . I know this."

"Thank you," Isla murmured.

"You're wonderful," Candace said enthusiastically. "You always know exactly what we would like. I'm so hungry I need potatoes! And here they are. Do you know, Stefano, Mr. Latterly and I climbed all the way up to the caldera?"

Stefano looked alarmed.

"No, no!" she said hastily. "Just up to the top of the mountainside. I wanted to go over and look in. Maybe I would have seen the fire in the center of the earth, boiling rock — red-hot like blood. Do you think? But I didn't, I promise." She took some of the crispy potatoes. "Have you ever looked into it, Stefano? Please, tell me the truth. Is it boiling rock down there? Like the middle of the earth?"

He looked at her with pleasure and a bright light of conspiracy in his eyes. "Yes, I did, once when I was young and very foolish . . ."

"And . . . ?" she asked breathlessly.

"And it was crimson as blood," he told her, ignoring everyone else at the table. "It throbbed, like a living heart . . ."

Isla looked alarmed. Bretherton put his hand on her arm very gently, as if he hardly dared to do it. She did not move even an inch, nor did she look at him, but there was the very smallest smile on her lips.

"Go on!" Candace burst out, urging Stefano to continue.

He gave an exaggerated shrug. "It sent up a cloud of steam, very, very hot. I turned and ran for my life!" Then he burst into laughter till the tears ran down his cheeks.

"You're teasing me," Candace protested.

"No, I'm not," he denied. "Once I was as young as you are, and just as curious." Then suddenly he was serious. "But I knew the strength of the mountain. I have seen it throw fire and rock up into the air and seen the lava flow till all the grass and the bushes burn and the people gather up their children and run as fast as they can down to the sea."

"And you rebuild this house every time?" Quinn asked, a touch sarcastically.

Stefano regarded him with disapproval, as if he had exhibited bad manners at the table, which indeed he had.

"No, Signor Quinn. My great-grandfather took care where to build these houses in the first place. The lava does not come this way.

Only sometimes hot rocks . . . on fire."

"I'm glad to hear that." Finbar looked at him warmly. "I have no wish to feel the mountain's displeasure. The fish is superb, Stefano. We are enjoying it very much. You are a master of this art."

Stefano smiled, accepting the compliment, and went back to the kitchen.

"Do you think he's right?" Isla asked no one in particular.

"Of course he is," Bretherton said quickly. "If his great-grandfather built this place, then there is every reason to believe him, and none at all to doubt."

"It probably won't erupt at all while we are here, anyway," Candace said in the silence that followed. She sounded rather disappointed.

The fish had been removed and the surprise dessert served when Walker-Bailey finally staggered in. He was filthy: his clothes were torn and stained with earth, dust, and what looked like blood. His hat was gone, his hair caked with dirt and sweat, and he was limping. He was clearly in a vile temper.

"Didn't wait for me, I see!" he snarled. "Could have been dead, for all any of you cared!" He looked at Isla as he said it.

She pushed her chair back and stood.

Candace turned to Bailey, her eyes wide. Without appearing to be aware of it, she reached out her hand and put it on Finbar's wrist gently.

"You appear to be hurt, Mr. Bailey," she said calmly. "Did you fall down coming home in the dark?" She spoke with much concern, but her choice of words suggested it was his own fault.

Charles winced. He could see in Bailey's face the way he had read the remark.

"You're hurt!" Isla said anxiously, before he could respond. "We must clean your wounds and bandage them in case they become infected. Stefano will put something by for you to eat later." She moved toward him nervously.

Bailey waved his hand to keep her

away, as if her ministrations irritated him. He glared at Candace.

"No, I did not fall over on my way home in the dark, young woman. I was attacked. Just as the sun was setting. Someone tried to kill me!" He stopped, allowing the horror and amazement to soak into the room.

"Kill you?" Finbar said in amazement. It was not possible to tell from his voice whether he believed Bailey or not.

"They didn't do a very good job of it," Candace whispered to Charles.

Charles tried to look stern and, knowing he'd failed, put his napkin up to his mouth. Please heaven Bailey did not look at him!

"That's terrible." Candace tried to sound sympathetic.

"Have you any idea who it was?" Finbar asked him.

"No idea at all," Bailey said bitterly. "It could have been any of you!"

Isla looked dreadfully pale. "That's an awful thing to say!" she protested. "Why on earth would you think it was any of us?"

"Because we know him," Candace replied. Then realizing how that sounded, she colored bright pink with annoyance at herself and embarrassment.

Bailey glared at her, but he was too furious to speak immediately.

Charles tried to rescue the situation. "Were you robbed, Mr. Bailey?" He thought it more likely that the man had fallen but was too ashamed to admit it.

"Your watch, perhaps?" Quinn asked, his face perfectly composed. If there was a shred of sarcasm in him, he did not reveal it.

Bailey chose to ignore him.

"They did not need to half kill me simply to pick my pocket!" he snapped, but at all of them except Quinn, toward whom he kept his back turned.

"You are quite right," Charles said soberly. "It looks as if you were unpleasantly injured, and it could have been much worse. Maybe you were stronger than they assumed?"

"Much," Bailey agreed. "Many people have made that mistake."

He glanced over toward Bretherton. "People tend to imagine that because they are taller, they are also stronger."

"Was he taller?" Charles asked, and then wondered why he was doing so. He was the latest arrival, the last in command, so to speak. But no one else seemed to be overly concerned. Either they did not know what to say or — on the other hand — they did not really want to know who was responsible. Or worse than that, perhaps they already knew. Was that possible? Could one of the people sitting here at this charming dinner table have crept up on Bailey in the dark and struck him down so that he was injured in the fall, his clothes torn and his legs bleeding?

If he had fallen some time ago, higher up the mountain, barely at dusk, then it was possible. They had all been alone, except for him and Candace.

Bailey looked around at them all, considering them one by one. "I don't know," he said at last. "He had the advantage of surprise. I was deep in thought and did not hear him on the soft ground. He struck suddenly, and very hard." He appeared somewhat mollified that at least someone was listening to him.

"A very vicious attack," Finbar said, more to himself than to Bailey. "How unpleasant for you. And you are certain you have no idea who it was?"

"Didn't I already say that?" Bailey demanded. "And spare me your false sympathy. I know far too much about you and your pretenses. I think you'd be pleased if you were certain I could never tell any of your friends, even accidentally."

Finbar looked straight at him. "You don't do much by accident, Bailey, except perhaps fall over."

Bailey's face was scarlet. "You won't get out of it that easily . . ."

Candace could take it no longer. She stood up abruptly. "You have no right to say that, Mr. Bailey. Uncle Roger isn't the only person here who doesn't like you. But we are civilized people and we don't go around attacking one another. If we did, you wouldn't have had to wait so long!" Her face gave away that she knew perfectly well she was breaking every rule of good manners, and didn't care. No one attacked one of her own and got away with it.

Bailey drew in his breath to reply, but Isla interrupted him.

"You really must come and let me tend to your wounds, dear. They look quite serious. At least we should stop the bleeding." Her voice trembled a little, as if she were frightened. Charles thought that actually Bailey's dignity was wounded more deeply than his body. The blood seemed to be dry already, as if he had been cut a couple of hours ago, and not so deeply that the bleeding had not stopped of its own accord.

Bailey put out his hand to fend her off, and she stopped, uncertain what to do.

"I've put up with it this long," he said harshly. "I'll survive another few minutes. I want to know who attacked me! Surely you can understand that?"

"Of course," Quinn observed with a gesture that was more a baring of the teeth than a smile. "They may do it again, since apparently they did not succeed very well this time."

Bailey looked at him icily. "I wouldn't put it past any of you, but you have the best motive — don't you?"

Quinn flushed hotly, but refused to back down. "Since I don't know anybody else's motive, I couldn't say." He was speaking only to Bailey and as if no one else in the room were listening.

Charles found his body aching with tension. What had been an easy, charming evening until Bailey's arrival had turned into something not only bitter but possibly even dangerous. To begin with he had thought Bailey absurd, but perhaps he was not. Maybe he had reason to fear.

Bailey seemed to be aware only of Quinn. "I always thought you were too damn stupid to understand Lucy," he said between his teeth. "Not a shred of imagination, have you? I know you too well, just as I know old Finbar. I don't know Bretherton, but there's nothing there anyway — beyond a stuffed uniform and a pathetic lust after my wife . . ."

Bretherton moved to protest, but the table was in the way and all he succeeded in doing was banging his knees on one of the legs and rattling the china.

Bailey gave him a withering look.

Isla was close to tears with anger and embarrassment.

"You missed me," Charles pointed out to him. "Why would I attack you? Simply that you're a cad doesn't seem to be enough. Admittedly, the house rests easier without you, but we're all here for only a short time."

"Unless one of you kills me first!" Bailey was angry, but this time Charles heard fear in his voice as well. Quite suddenly, in an instant, it all changed. Until then he had been assuming that Bailey had tripped in the dark, and was using it as a chance to attack all of them and become the center of attention.

"You are quite right, Mr. Bailey," he said aloud. "We are making light of it because it is a very frightening idea, and we don't want it to be true. We were assuming it was an accident, and there was no malice intended. But if, as you say, it was deliberate, then the whole picture alters and becomes very grave indeed." He chose the word intentionally, and was rewarded by an instant of real fear in Bailey's eyes.

That look, there and then gone again in less than a second, changed Charles's mind. Walker-Bailey was afraid. His anger covered something close to panic inside him. Charles should have felt pity and was not proud of himself that he didn't.

"Perhaps you had better go and have your wounds attended to," he suggested more gently. Finbar rose to his feet. "I think I'll excuse myself also," he said quietly. "It has been a long day. Good night, Mrs. Bailey." He inclined his head toward Bretherton and Quinn, and then to Charles.

Candace stood also, looking curiously at her uncle, then turned to leave. Charles walked beside her, a few steps after Finbar. There was an inexpressible weariness in the old man's movements.

Candace stood next to Charles for a moment.

"Do you really think someone pushed him?" she asked, her voice very low. "And please don't lie to me."

"I don't know," he said, and he was absolutely honest. "But I think he believes so. He could just have slipped in the dark."

"He's so horrible I wouldn't blame someone, would you?" she asked.

"You have to have a very dreadful reason to want to kill anyone," he said seriously. "Trying to scare him, I can understand. But it really is dangerous to push a man over in the dark, on that lava. He could have hit his head, and that would have been the end of him."

"Colonel Bretherton's in love with Mrs. Bailey, you know," she told him.

He thought of arguing, but she would only think he was evading the truth.

"Yes, I think so," he agreed.

"I wouldn't blame her if she'd pushed him," Candace went on. "He's horrible to her, no matter how hard she tries to please him. If it was she, and I found out, I wouldn't tell anyone."

He felt a sudden chill of real fear.

"You must, Candace. If you know anything you must share it."

"Why? He's horrible! I wouldn't hurt him! But I wouldn't tell on anyone else who did." There was certainty and defiance in her face and in the rigid angles of her body.

He caught her shoulder. It was slender, the bones fine.

"Candace! Maybe you wouldn't hurt him, but he might very well hurt you if he thought you knew something."

She stared at him.

"How would your uncle manage without you?" he said. "Have you thought of that?"

"No," she agreed in a whisper. "I'll be careful, I promise!"

"Good. I believe you. Now go to

bed and don't get up until tomorrow morning."

She smiled. "Yes, Charles."

Charles was tired after the long
climb up the mountain, and then
the tension at dinner. He was asleep
within ten minutes of putting out
the light.

He woke up with his heart pounding but no idea what had disturbed
him. It was still dark. He could
barely make out the shape of the
window, which was just a little
paler than the walls.

Had he been dreaming? He could
recall nothing, but then most
dreams slipped away within moments.

Then he heard it again: a sharp,

cracking sound that seemed to fill the air and be all around him, as if it came from every direction. He sat upright in bed, muscles knotted, body aching with the strain. But what was it? It was too loud, too all-pervasive to be any kind of gun.

Thunder?

There was a low rumbling sound, as of someone rolling a heavy cart over a stony road, but far louder.

Now, bone-deep, he knew what it was. The mountain was awakening. Deep in the caldera the lava was boiling up, shaking the earth, seeking escape from its long imprisonment beneath the surface.

Trembling, he climbed out of the bed and put on his dressing gown.

He fumbled with the ties. His fingers were awkward, and all the time he was listening for another crack, another sound that would tell him what was happening.

Why? There was nothing he could do about it.

He opened the door and went outside into the still night air. It smelled a little different, more acrid. Or was that his imagination? There was no light except for that from a very fitful moon. No red glare of flames. He looked toward the mountain, but there was nothing to see except a heavier, denser blackness where it loomed over them, filling the sky. There were no flames, no scarlet rivers of molten rock.

Perhaps he was making a fuss over nothing very much. It had stirred in its sleep, that was all. A summer thunderstorm might make such noises and, with lightning strikes, probably do more damage. He was making a fool of himself. Not a good example to set.

He turned to go back to his room, glad no one had seen him.

"Signor? Signor Latterly?"

He recognized Stefano's voice the moment before he saw him in the gloom, just a deeper shadow.

"Stefano? Are you all right?"

"Of course." Stefano's voice was low, confident, but there was a note in it that Charles had not heard before. Anxiety? Or just concern for his guests?

"Did the mountain disturb you?" Stefano went on. "I am sorry. Sometimes it makes a noise. Don't let it worry you."

"I don't see anything." Charles was still facing the mountain, searching for signs of smoke in the sky, a red glow of fire reflected on the clouds above.

"Maybe some fire later." Stefano was close beside him now. "It shake a little bit. Just want to see nothing has fallen, broken on the ground, you know? Don't want anyone not looking carefully, and trip."

"You mean like Bailey?" Charles said with a wry smile.

"He is an unhappy one, that," Stefano said sadly.

"And determined to make the rest

of us the same," Charles agreed.

"I am sorry . . ." Stefano sounded as if he felt he was to blame.

"It's not your fault," Charles assured him.

"I let him come. This is my house. I want all of you to be happy here. Is good. Is peace. Christmas coming. Time of hope, for everyone." Stefano was smiling in the darkness, Charles could tell that from the sound of his words, but there was unease in them, too. Was that caused by Walker-Bailey or the mountain?

"Go back to bed, Signor Latterly," Stefano urged him. "I think there is nothing broken. It was only a little shake. But I make sure. Please, go back to sleep. In the morning it will all be quiet again. Rest, so you can go for a long walk tomorrow, perhaps the other way. You see different sights, yes?"

Charles could hear the pleading in his voice.

"Yes," he agreed. "Good idea. In every direction there are beautiful things to see. Good night, Stefano."

"Good night, signor. Sleep well."

Charles was awoken the second time by an insistent knocking on his door. He opened his eyes and saw that daylight was just beginning to break. There was a pallor to the sky through the window.

The knocking was repeated.

He climbed out of bed, seized his robe, and went to the door.

Roger Finbar stood just outside. He was fully dressed, but looked hastily so. He had no tie on, and his jacket was a trifle rumpled and unfastened. His hair was untidy, as if he had made only a perfunctory attempt to brush it.

But it was his face that arrested Charles's attention. Even in the dim light of the dawn, he looked haggard and very frail.

"Come in," Charles said immediately, bracing himself to catch the man's weight if he should collapse.

"Thank you," Finbar accepted and followed him inside. His voice was perfectly steady, but what effort that required of him could only be guessed. He sat in the one chair in the room, and Charles sat on the end of the bed, opposite him.

"Are you all right, sir?" Charles asked anxiously. "Is there anything I can do to help?" He had no idea what that might be, but he found himself wishing profoundly that there would be something.

"Yes, there is," Finbar said with a wry smile. "That is why I have come to disturb you at this rather uncivil hour. I am not sure if I will have another chance. I think no one knows what this day will bring."

"No one ever knows the future," Charles pointed out. "Or do you mean this day in particular?"

Finbar gave a slight nod; in the slowly broadening light it was visible only in a shifting of the shadows.

"I mean it of this day in particular."

"If you are thinking of that ass Bailey, then don't worry about him." Charles tried to sound assured, although he wasn't. He was anxious himself about what further trouble Bailey would cause.

Finbar made a slight gesture of dismissal with one hand. "Oh, Bailey is a wretched man, and no doubt the cause of a great deal of unnecessary misery, but I was thinking of something quite unstoppable that not even Bailey can affect in the slightest."

Charles did not interrupt with a question.

"Did you hear the mountain in

the night?" Finbar asked, his eyes searching Charles's face as much as he could in the dim light.

"Yes," Charles said warily. "I woke once. I think it was a particularly loud crash and then a sort of rumbling, rather the way a house does if it is set too close to the railway track and a heavy train passes by. I looked, but I couldn't see anything. Could it have been a rockfall? Does it do that? Higher up, some of the slopes seem loose, like scree."

"I don't know," Finbar admitted, "but it has been rumbling most of the night. In spite of all assurances to the contrary, I think we are going to have a real eruption with lava flow, bombs, and —"

"Bombs?" Charles could not hide his alarm.

The light was now broad enough for Charles to see the smile on Finbar's face. "Small lumps of lava, molten rock, and gas that fly up in the air out of the crater and land anywhere within a few miles, depending on size and the violence with which they are hurled. They explode whenever they hit something, much as a bomb would. They set fire to anything combustible, such as grass or the brush on the mountainsides."

"Oh." It was an acknowledgment. He should have realized it. "What is it you think I can do? That seems like a convulsion of the earth beyond any human intervention at all."

"Of course it is," Finbar agreed quietly. "But if the fires are too bad, the heat too intense, then we will all leave here and make for the sea, as fast as we can. I will do my best, but I'm afraid I have nothing like the strength I used to have. I'm slow. I falter and could fall. I want you to promise that if anything happens to me, you will look after Candace. She has no one else. I am the last of her family. She needs more than a roof over her head in some distant relative's house, until they can marry her off to someone they consider suitable."

The very idea of it revolted Charles. Such a situation would crush the joy out of Candace.

"I see that you find the idea repellent," Finbar said softly. "You can see the spark in her. And I know she likes you. She will trust you, and if you are honest and gentle with her, she will love you for it. Before you refuse, consider what the alternative is for her, please?"

He would not beg, but Charles could see the depth of emotion in his face, even in this pallid light. His instinct was to refuse, to tell Finbar what a failure he had made of his own life. If the old man had any idea how feeble, how directionless Charles was, he would never entrust him with such a task. He surely had nothing in his life as precious to him as that child!

"We'll get you down the mountain," he said. "That is, if it does erupt. Stefano has lived here all his life, and he doesn't seem to think it will."

"Charles," Finbar said very quietly, "you know as well as I do that Stefano puts on a front for all of our comfort. Maybe it won't blow, but maybe it will. I've heard it rumbling all night. The strength of it is building. I only ask you to promise me that if anything happens to me, you will not let Candace stay and try to help me, and get burned to death or crushed." He gave a very slight smile. "Perhaps the volcano is only complaining in its sleep, and it will all be quiet again in a few hours. We will stay here over Christmas, and then

Bailey and poor Isla will go back to some nice home that he has chosen, and she hates. Bretherton will go back to his home, and try to forget her, and of course he will fail. Quinn will continue to pretend to be writing another book, which of course he will not do, because he did not write the first one."

"What do you mean, 'he did not write the first one'?" Charles asked, shocked.

Finbar shook his head. "He took the credit, but the passion is someone else's," he replied.

"Who else?" Charles was disturbed by the thought. "You mean someone else told him the stories?"

"Probably something like that." Finbar dismissed the subject. "All I meant was that life will go back to normal. You will return to London and whatever it is you do, Candace and I will go back to our lives. Stefano will have new guests. The mountain will go back to sleep again."

It sounded terribly final, and in a way like a kind of failure, something attempted and not achieved, searched for and not found.

"Of course I will look after her if anything happens," Charles said, hearing his own voice as if it belonged to a stranger. "And you," he added. "They say Stromboli is always erupting, but that it is never serious."

"I hope so," Finbar agreed. He held out his hand, offering it to

Charles.

Charles took a deep breath, and then clasped it. It was the making of an agreement, the sealing of a promise, and he knew it. But surely it would never be needed? The mountain would go back to its habitual silence. Finbar would benefit from his holiday, and this would all be a memory. But the gesture was a kindness at six o'clock on a winter morning, after a disturbed night.

Finbar rose to his feet a little stiffly and Charles stood as well, as courtesy required.

"Thank you," Finbar said softly. "I will see you at breakfast."

Breakfast was unusually subdued.

Stefano came out of the kitchen with his usual smile, but he spoke very little, and it was only about the food. Did everyone have sufficient? Was the bread to their taste? And the goat cheese and the ham? Everyone agreed that it was, and thanked him.

Isla drew in breath once and began to ask how everybody was, then stopped halfway through. It seemed they had all heard the mountain in the night. Comments were begun, and then abandoned. No one wished to put voice to what might happen next, until Walker-Bailey said what they had all been thinking.

"Bit of a surprise, isn't it?" he said to Charles. "Wasn't expecting so much noise in the night. Closer to the damn thing than I realized. Still, this house has been here for generations, possibly centuries. I daresay it gets the occasional scar, but nothing serious. I suggest no one climbs today."

"I'm sure no one was going to," Quinn said to him, then took the last piece of bread out of the basket. He reached for the jam.

Just as he pushed the spoon into it, there was a deafening crash and then a roar that seemed to fill the air. He dropped the spoon on the cloth and went sheet white.

"God Almighty!" Bailey said in a high voice.

Isla opened her mouth but made no sound at all.

"Everybody, keep calm," Brether-ton ordered, as if he were in charge of a military platoon under fire.

Candace took Finbar's hand, but she did not move. Perhaps beside him was the safest place she could imagine.

There was another roar and red light filled the room, although it was long past the blazing winter sunrise. It remained for seconds . . . nine or ten . . . although it seemed like an age. Finally it died and there was only a distant grumbling.

"Thank God!" Quinn said, letting out his breath.

There was the sound of an explosion, perhaps a hundred yards away, loud as a blast of dynamite.

"Bombs!" Charles cried out. "Under the table!"

"Bombs under the table?" Quinn said incredulously. "Have you lost your wits, man?"

"Lava bombs!" Charles shouted at him. "From the volcano . . . Get under the table. It'll protect you at least a bit, if the ceiling comes in."

"Don't be absurd!" Quinn retaliated.

Bretherton took Isla by the hand and pulled her off her seat. "Do as Latterly says!" he ordered. "There'll be more." And as she all but fell onto the floor on her hands and knees, there was another crash of exploding lava bombs not more than fifty yards away.

Candace pulled Finbar off his seat, and both of them scrambled under the table as well.

There was another great roar of sound, drowning everything else, and then a tremendous crash as if part of the earth had been torn open. Red light filled the room again.

Now everyone was under the table. It had seemed quite large when they sat around it, but with their entire bodies cramped between the four legs they were tangled with one another in a forced intimacy all of them would have preferred not to know. Charles was closest to Candace and Finbar, but Bretherton's foot was next to his thigh, and he had to double up uncomfortably to avoid his own feet poking Isla Bailey. Walker-

Bailey was so averse to the whole idea that only his head and chest were actually under the table, his legs extended completely into the room. Quinn was bent forward, knees drawn up to his chest.

Only Stefano was missing, and that worried Charles. He, of all of them, was the one man who understood the dangers of flying rocks and the explosive nature of the gases inside the lava.

"This is absurd!" Walker-Bailey said angrily. "I didn't come here to spend my Christmas crouching under a table with a bunch of strangers."

"Well, if you wanted to do it with friends you should have brought them with you!" Bretherton told him.

"You could always leave," Candace suggested hopefully.

But it was Charles who backed out carefully, trying not to crack his head on the table frame. "I'm going to find Stefano," he told them.

"What on earth do you imagine he can do about it?" Quinn asked derisively. "It's the volcano, man! Not even God can stop the bloody thing!"

"I'm not expecting him to do anything about it," Charles snapped back at him. "I want to make sure he's all right! He might be hurt somewhere, and needing help, while we're all crushed under here in safety." He stood up, looking around him. Nothing appeared to be damaged, but through the window facing the mountain he could see the sky was sullen red. There was a lot of smoke constantly billowing, changing shape as more ash was added to it. He could smell it in the air, acrid, stinging his eyes.

"What's happening?" Quinn demanded.

"A lot of ash and dust," Charles replied. "I can't see anything broken."

"Good. False alarm." Quinn unfolded himself clumsily and stood up, too, and the moment after Walker-Bailey came out also.

Charles walked over to the door and pulled it open.

Outside was less awful than he

had feared. There was a fine film of either dust or ash over everything, and the smell of burned grass, but no damage to the structure of the building that he could see.

He walked a little farther, calling out Stefano's name. It was another twenty yards before he heard an answer, and finally came across Stefano standing in front of the chicken coop with a hammer in one hand and nails in the other.

"You should be inside, Signor Latterly," he said reprovingly. "It isn't finished yet." He glanced beyond Charles at the mountain, now half hidden by enormous plumes of smoke and ash towering into the sky.

"You think there'll be more?"

Charles asked him.

Stefano frowned. "I have no reason, I just feel it. Maybe the smell of it is different, I don't know. But it is Stromboli; it will never completely finish, nor will it blow the whole island up, like Vesuvius. Not even as bad as Etna. But one thing above all, it will keep no rules. It will do as it pleases. No warning. At least none that we understand. And I have been here, my family, for centuries. But I do not trust the old devil. It will quiet soon, then we will go down to the sea . . . for a while. Safer there."

Almost as he finished speaking they were deafened by a crack like thunder from near the top of the mountain, and a great gout of fire shot high into the air. It must have been a thousand pieces of molten rock — ten thousand — but it looked like a sheet of fire arced into the sky, brilliant in color even through the smoke. Then it began to fall like burning rain, but far away on the southern side, so they did not see it land.

Stefano shook his head. "Go back inside, Mr. Latterly," he said gravely.

Charles did not move. "What are you doing with the chickens?"

Stefano sighed. "I think I let them go. Best they look after themselves." He put the nails back into the loose pocket of his trousers. "If I shut them in, and it comes this way, they burn. Or they get bad fright and hurt themselves trying to get out." Then he spoke to the chickens, in Italian, as if they would understand what he said. He propped the coop door open and, blinking a little, put his hand on Charles's arm and led him back toward the house.

"We go into the cellar now. Is safer there. When it is quieter, we all go down the mountain toward the sea. Stromboli never rain fire that far. Even the worst lava stop when it reach the water. Come. I have food prepared. And water. It take us a little while to get that far."

Obediently Charles went with him. He realized for the first time that Stefano was frightened of the mountain. It was not love he felt for it but respect, awe, and that included a knowledge of its power. He lived with it as a sailor does with the sea. Its grandeur was dangerous, compelling, and in a way it was beautiful, but only a fool took any part of it for granted. It gave life, but it also dealt death.

They were all glad to see Stefano, perhaps as much feeling relief that he was there to look after them as pleasure that he was unharmed. He shepherded them to the cellar, a deep cool place beneath the main house where a vast quantity of wine was stored.

They had gone through a hatch-way down a long flight of steps, so Charles was aware that it was far under the ground. There were two entrances as a precaution against getting trapped below.

Stefano looked around at them. "Where is Mr. Bailey?" he asked.

"Late, as always," Quinn replied before anyone else could.

"I thought he was behind us! Do you think he might be hurt?" Isla said, alarmed. "The gashes on his leg last night were quite deep."

"It didn't stop him walking around," Colonel Bretherton said with a scowl. "He just can't bear taking orders, even for everyone's safety."

"I'll go and look for the damn fool," Quinn offered. "He can't be far."

No one argued with him. Isla shot him a look of surprise and gratitude.

Bretherton swore under his breath. "Damn fool!" he said, worry sharpening his tone. He turned to Stefano. "Do you think the mountain has stopped, and he sees no need for this?"

"No, the mountain has not stopped," Stefano answered without hesitation. "It is building up. I think it will be quite . . . quite large." He bit his lip with regret that he had said so much.

Finbar and Candace were sitting together. The guests could all see each other, but only dimly, by the light of two lanterns Stefano kept in the cellar for searching the wine racks, and doing the occasional sweeping and tidying necessary. There were additional candle supplies, he assured them.

"Good God!" Bretherton exclaimed. "How long do you think we are going to be down here?"

"I think when there is a lull in the volcano's anger, we should go up and look. If it is safe, we should make our way down to the sea."

"How?" Isla asked with a frown. "The pony and trap went back down once it had brought us here."

"We will walk, signora," Stefano answered. "It is not so very far. It will take us a few hours, but we can rest on the way."

Isla looked aghast at the idea.

"We'll walk together," Candace said quickly. "We'll all help one another. Don't worry . . ."

There was a sound of wood banging somewhere above them, and then the hatch opened and daylight shone on the steps. A moment later the hatch closed and they heard feet on the steps.

"Walker?" Isla rose to her feet, relief flooding her face.

Charles could not help wondering if she really was pleased to see him, or if she was wise enough to act as if she were. If she failed to show what he considered the appropriate reactions, she might pay for it for a long time. He wondered how anyone endured such a marriage. Perhaps she believed that she had given her word in church, and only death would release her from it.

But it was not Bailey who reached

the bottom of the steps and came into the light of the nearest lantern, it was Quinn, carrying several folded blankets.

"There are some nasty bits of rock flying around, and some of it is actual lava, hot as hell. Sets fire to the grass." He sat down a couple of feet away from Isla.

"Did you see Bailey?" Charles asked him.

Quinn raised his eyebrows. "I couldn't find him. I stopped to get these." He gestured to the blankets with a slight shrug. "I expect he'll be here any moment." He dismissed the subject and turned to Stefano. "How long do you think this will go on for? It doesn't look too bad up there. I suppose you have to be careful; we are more or less your responsibility. I can see that. But surely in an hour or two . . ." He stopped because another volley of sound cut him off. Even here, as far below the ground as they were, they could hear the noise and feel a tremor in the earth around them as another shower of rocks, or bombs, struck close to where they were.

Stefano crossed himself and closed his eyes.

Charles felt deeply sorry for him. It must be one of his worst nightmares, to be stuck in the cellar with a group of frightened and largely thankless guests, while the volcano bombarded his home, the house his ancestors had built, probably been born in and died in. He wondered for an instant if the chickens had gone.

Stefano rose to his feet. It clearly cost him some effort.

"What is it?" Quinn demanded. "Can we go out now?"

"No, Signor Quinn, you cannot," Stefano replied. "We all stay here until there is no more explosions. Then we will go down to the sea."

"Ridiculous!" Quinn said tartly. "You're making too much of it, man. The cellar is fine. When was the last time it ever caved in, I ask you!"

"We will go down to the sea," Stefano repeated, not even looking at Quinn. "Now I must go to find Mr. Bailey. It is not safe up there."

He walked toward the bottom of the cellar steps.

"Wait!" Charles stood up also. "Do it in half the time with two of us. And it will be safer."

"Not very logical," Quinn commented. "If you go separately, you're no help, and if you go together, you won't be any faster."

Charles swung round angrily and glared at Quinn. "And if you had brought Bailey down instead of watching him from a distance, it wouldn't be necessary. Now sit still and shut up!" He followed Stefano up the steps without turning back to see how Quinn had dealt with the verbal attack. Frankly, he did not care.

Stefano opened the hatch and

went out, Charles on his heels.

Outside he stared around in amazement. The towers of ash in the sky were far larger, billowing as he watched them, growing, roiling as if they were almost solid, great whirlpools, folding in on themselves and then swelling outward again as if they meant to darken the whole sky. He saw lightning fork through them, and then another jet of scarlet fire hundreds of feet high. At the same moment the ground below his feet trembled and the roar of it drowned any words he might have had.

Stefano jerked his head to indicate the way they should go, and Charles followed him quickly. He had no wish whatever to be caught out here alone.

They searched the house, looking in all the public rooms and then the bedrooms. Stefano had the keys and it took only a glance in each to know that Bailey was not there. All the time the mountain rumbled sporadically. The air was thick with the stench of ash and sulfur, burned grass, and the dust of stone where pieces of wall had been struck by lumps of burning lava and left scorched and, in many places, broken.

It was probably mendable. Perhaps this was the price of living on this amazing island, but Charles grieved for the damage, the carefully nurtured buildings and gardens that had been ruined in a few moments.

They started on the outbuildings, storerooms, and garden sheds. Here the damage was worse. These buildings were only a few dozen yards closer to the mountain, but perhaps they had been built here originally as the first wall of defense.

The first Charles and Stefano looked in was the one most seriously damaged. One side of the roof had completely collapsed, rafters and tiles having fallen in. The upper edges of the supporting walls were scarred with fire where flying lava had struck them with tremendous force.

It was inside the wreck of this room that they found Walker-

Bailey's body. He was lying on the floor on his back, a rafter from the damaged ceiling fallen across his chest. Blood covered his shoulders and pooled on the floor behind the back of his head.

Stefano said something in Italian. Charles did not know the words, but he certainly understood the sentiment. He would have said something the same if his mouth was not too dry to speak at all, and his heart pounding as if to drown out all other sounds.

Stefano bent to touch the wrist of one of the outflung arms. His own hand was shaking so hard he had to make a deliberate effort to force himself to be still. It was more than a minute before he looked up at

Charles, his face ashen under his olive skin.

"I am sorry, but he is dead." He closed his eyes. "Now how are we going to tell the signora? Poor creature . . ."

Charles held out his hand and helped Stefano to his feet. He was surprised how much of his weight he had to take.

"It's not your fault, Stefano," he said. "If the stupid man had come in with the rest of us, he would be all right. I'm sure she'll be shaken up. I daresay she wouldn't have wished him dead. But on the other hand, I rather think she will recover."

Stefano looked wretched.

"He was not a nice man," he

agreed. "Now he has died without the chance to do better. That is very sad, Mr. Latterly. In fact, perhaps it is the last tragedy in a man's life. I fear he will not be much missed."

"I'll go and tell them," Charles offered. The instant the words were out of his mouth he wondered what on earth had made him say them. But the warmth that now filled Stefano's face made them impossible to take back. He had no idea how he was going to make it any easier for the others than Stefano would. Perhaps his offer stemmed from gratitude for Stefano's warmth, the kindness he had shown, his love of simple things like good bread, and the welcome he had shown his guests.

"I will check the rest of the damage, perhaps," Stefano started to speak again. "I . . . I think the mountain is going to get worse before it quiets down. Don't let them argue with you, Mr. Latterly. They must be ready to leave at the first opportunity. I will recognize it and tell them. I know the way down. We have had to leave before."

"But the house is fine!" Charles protested, indicating it by spreading his arms apart in both directions.

"Of course it is," Stefano agreed. "No one was ever killed, because they respect the mountain. They know when to leave. Now, please, if your offer is to tell them of Mr.

Bailey's sad going, then do so. Otherwise I will do it, of course."

"No," Charles said quickly. "It's better I do. And anyway, you need to make things ready for us when we can leave . . . if you think that after the next lull it will really get worse?"

"I do," Stefano said with a slight nod. "I'm afraid I do. Thank you, my friend."

Charles turned to go, but had gone no farther than a dozen yards when he saw Finbar coming toward him. He was walking with a slight limp, as if he had injured himself, and now his whole body was stiff.

Charles increased his pace. "Are you all right?" he said with anxiety.

"Yes, yes," Finbar assured him. "I

came to see if you needed assistance. Where is Stefano? Did you find Bailey? He is a most objectionable man but we can't leave him behind."

"I'm afraid we will have to," Charles answered grimly.

Finbar did not understand. "No, Latterly, we can't. I agree he is a most unpleasant creature, and I have no desire to see him again once we reach safety, but whatever he is, or is not, we are not people who leave anyone behind in a situation like this. I —"

Charles interrupted him. "He's dead. I'm sorry to put it so very bluntly, but we haven't time for pleasantries. Stefano thinks that after a lull or two the mountain may really blow. When we have the chance, we must make our way down the mountain toward the sea. We will have enough trouble walking all that way. It is several miles, and we have women . . . at least, Mrs. Bailey. I think she will not find it easy, and may need help. But we cannot take a dead body with us, even if we could free him from where he's trapped."

"I suppose you are quite sure he's dead?" Finbar said, his face pale.

"Stefano is. But if you want to make certain for yourself, he's in the outbuilding just back there." He turned and pointed.

"Trapped?"

"Yes. A good part of the ceiling came in and one of the beams fell across his chest."

"I see." Finbar started moving again stiffly. He walked past Charles toward the outbuilding.

Charles turned and followed him. They went inside. It was exactly as Charles had left it, except that Stefano was not there.

"Oh dear," Finbar said, regarding the body of Walker-Bailey splayed out on the floor. "Yes, I see what you mean. Excuse me." He went over to the body and kneeled down beside it. He appeared to consider it for some time. He bent farther forward and looked very closely at the beam.

"If we try moving it, I think we may well bring more of the roof down on ourselves," Charles said simply. "It all looks as if it could cave in with another shift of anything."

Finbar looked up at the ceiling. "I think you are correct. But that is not what concerns me, Charles." He said Charles's given name as easily as if they had known each other for years. "Come here. I think you need to see this."

Reluctantly Charles went several steps closer to the body. Without life in it, it looked rather smaller than it had a few hours ago, puffed up by self-righteousness and anger. Now there was nothing left at all, just a small, wiry man whose soul was already somewhere far off, leaving behind only emptiness.

"This," Finbar said quietly. Even

the mountain had fallen temporarily silent. There was no roar, no crack of rocks, as if it had also stopped breathing.

"What am I looking at?" Charles asked.

Finbar pointed to the pool of blood beneath Bailey's head. It extended from the side of his head where it was matted on the scalp above the ear, right down to his shoulder on that side.

"Not a lot of blood for a scalp wound," Finbar observed.

"Looks like a lot to me," Charles said unhappily. "He must have been struck by the beam very hard."

"Bend down farther," Finbar told him, lowering his own head to demonstrate just what he meant.

Reluctantly, Charles obeyed. That was when he saw the jagged flap of skin falling open in Bailey's neck. The cut was not long, but it was filled with blood and was just above the beginning of the pool around him.

"I don't understand," he said, straightening up and staring at Finbar.

"Yes, you do," Finbar answered softly. "That is the wound that killed him, right across the artery. The head wound is slight."

Charles was puzzled, fighting off the truth. "I thought an arterial wound like that would bleed — catastrophically!"

"It would," Finbar agreed. "He

didn't die here. Somewhere else, probably not far away there is a piece of ground soaked with blood. But I daresay the dust and lava will hide it until long after we are gone. He was moved here, and it was made to look like an accidental death — just one more victim of the volcano."

Suddenly Charles was cold, far inside himself. That Walker-Bailey was dead was sad and disturbing. Much as he had disliked him, he would not have wished this for him. And that he had been killed deliberately, murdered, meant that someone else was also changed forever and, beyond that, they all would somehow have to deal with it. There was no escape from the conclusion that one of them in the house had done it. Apart from their group, who else even knew of Walker-Bailey, let alone cared whether he lived or died?

Charles stared at Finbar.

"I know," Finbar said quietly. "One of them did this. A blade to the throat could have been done by anyone. It doesn't take any particular strength and, given Bailey's size and probable weight, it wouldn't be too difficult to have dragged him here, once he couldn't fight back."

"Should we look for where he was killed?" Charles asked reluctantly.

Finbar was prevented from answering by another roar from the volcano and a deep rumble in the earth as everything around them trembled and more stone and plaster fell from the walls.

For several seconds it went on, and they both remained frozen to the spot. Finally it subsided and, with a bleak smile, Finbar rose to his feet.

"I think not," he said wryly. "It hardly matters. I am no expert in reading evidence from a pool of blood, and I doubt you are. It will not tell us which of them killed the man. I think we would be wise to leave here." He looked around him. "The structure has been damaged sufficiently; another shake and it could fall in on us."

As he spoke he led the way across the room, stepping carefully on the debris and making for the doorway out into the whirling dust and smoke.

Instinctively both of them turned to look back at the mountain. Its peak was now hidden by more smoke. It seemed to tower into the sky in dark, billowing clouds, always moving, swirling, turning in on itself like some giant whirlpool, and then exploding out again, always climbing. Looking at it now, Charles believed that Stefano was right. There was worse to come.

He looked at Finbar, and saw his own thoughts reflected in the other man's face.

Finbar stopped. "Charles . . . I asked you to look after Candace, if I should get lost, or delayed . . . or if something happened to me. I imagined it was only a brief consideration. In a couple of weeks Christmas will be long over, and we will all be in our homes again. Perhaps we will not meet after that."

"I will look after her," Charles assured him. He could see the fear in Finbar's face. What else could he say?

"And if I die?" Finbar asked, raising his voice only just enough to be heard above the distant roar of the volcano.

There was only one possible answer. Charles thought for an instant of pointing out that if they got caught in the eruption, then they would all die. But he knew that was not what Finbar was thinking of.

The old man knew his own physical limits were closing in on him more tightly every day. He was afraid of holding them all up in their escape because of his weakness. No one would ever think of leaving him behind.

No, that was not entirely true. Bretherton certainly wouldn't. Quinn he was less sure about. Quinn might feel it acceptable to go ahead with Isla and Candace, to save them. Except, of course, Candace wouldn't leave Finbar, no matter how much he wished her to. He must know her well enough to understand that to do it would haunt the rest of her life.

But there was no time for reasoned arguments when the answers were understood anyway.

"Of course I will," he said to Finbar. "I'll take her back to wherever she needs to be, and see that whoever is looking after her has at least some idea of what all this was like." He indicated the even more massive cloud that now filled half the sky.

Finbar grasped Charles's arm with his strong, thin hand.

"Charles, there is no one to care for her, talk to her, listen to her, guide her through the hard years ahead. I had hoped to do it, and I yet might, but I need to be certain that you will if . . . if I cannot." He took his hand off Charles's arm and held it out. He could not beg, but it was in his eyes, his face.

Charles hesitated only long enough to swallow hard. He was unworthy of this. Finbar did not know him at all. He saw only the man he had been these few days, and that Candace liked him. He did not know all the colorless years that had come before, the unhappiness gnawing at him in places hidden from others. But they were still there, the doubts, the fears, the unbelief. The whole edifice of his life that amounted to failure.

But here was an old man with one child dependent upon him, and he was afraid that he would die and leave her alone, without companionship or defense. There was only Charles for him to turn to.

Charles clasped his hand and

shook it, amazed at the strength in the old man. He had been a giant of some sort in his time, a leader, a man to trust. Charles wished passionately, with all the strength he had, that he were more like him.

"Yes, sir," he said firmly. "I will. Now, if you please, we need to go and tell the others that Walker-Bailey is dead, there is nothing we can do to help him, and the mountain is building up for a major eruption. Stefano will show us the safest way down the mountain to the sea."

Finbar clasped his hand a moment longer, then let go of it with a smile. "Thank you," was all he said.

They were not far from the house,

perhaps fifty yards, including the bends in the path around other buildings, but the ground was strewn with rubble, there were other beams down, and here and there some of the buildings were burning where they had been struck by bombs of burning lava.

They were only twenty yards away when Stefano came out of one of the sheds carrying a couple of heavy canvas rucksacks. He looked filthy and exhausted.

"Here," he said with a smile. "We can carry food in these. We will only need a little. But water, we must have water. Bandages in case someone gets burned." He held out one to Charles and kept the other. "Come . . ."

Charles took it and they began to walk the last few yards to the back door of the house.

Almost immediately there was a shattering noise from far up the mountain, so loud it seemed to reverberate around the sky. And a gout of flame shot into the air so vivid it burned scarlet even through the smoke, and lava spewed around it in ever-widening fountains of liquid fire.

Stefano pushed them toward the nearest wall, shielding them as much as he could.

Charles was knocked off his feet by a sudden tremendous impact. He collapsed to the ground, bruised, and aware the moment after of pain in both his legs. There was a scream, cut off horribly, then the smell of burning flesh.

Charles gasped for breath, trying to throw off the weight. For seconds he could barely breathe. He was suffocating with the pressure on his chest. It took every ounce of his strength not to panic. He could see something, then his eyes were covered with cloth, and more weight. The smell of burning was vile; it filled his nose and mouth, clogged his throat.

Then suddenly the pressure eased, the cloth came off his face. He gulped in air, but it was still full of the terrible taste.

Finbar was talking to him. He tried to concentrate on what he was saying.

"Charles! Charles, are you all right?"

"Yes," he croaked. "Yes, I think so." He wiped his hands over his eyes and found he could see. Finbar was lying beside him, propped on his elbow, his face smeared with ash and dust, but worse than that, with blood. His features were contorted with pain.

Charles struggled to sit up. He ached all over, but apart from a few scorches on his arms and legs he was unhurt. Then he saw Stefano, lying a few feet away. The side of his head was hideously burned; in fact, the cloth of his shirt was still smoldering. One of the lava bombs must have hit him directly.

Finbar's hand was gripping

Charles's arm weakly but perhaps as hard as he had power to do.

"Don't," he said softly, more a willing of the word than a sound. "He's dead, Charles. There's nothing we can do for him except pick up the job he would have done. He gave his life to save us. Now you must take the others down to the sea."

"But you . . ." Charles started, his voice choking, not on the ash or the smell of burned human flesh, but on his own grief.

"No," Finbar said without hesitation. "I can't make it. Both my legs are broken. You must go alone."

"I can't leave you!" Charles protested. It was unthinkable! Even without Candace, he couldn't have done that. Even if he had not cared for Finbar himself, liked the man, admired him deeply. "No!" he repeated.

"I can't come with you," Finbar repeated. "And I think I'm bleeding inside. It won't be long."

"I don't care! I'm not leaving you!"

"You gave me your word, Charles," Finbar reminded him. "If you stay here with me, I'll die anyway, and who will get the others down to the sea? The mountain isn't finished yet. Stefano knew that, and so do you."

"Colonel Bretherton . . ." Charles argued. "Probably better than I could anyway. He's a natural leader. Dammit, he's a colonel."

"You'll do it," Finbar said. He smiled slightly. He was visibly growing weaker.

Charles could feel the tears on his face running through the ash, and the grief choking him.

Finbar reached for his hand, but failed to clasp it as he sank backward.

Charles leaned over and held Finbar's hand for an instant. Then, unable to look at him any longer, he lurched to his feet to keep his promise.

Barely maintaining his self-control, completely unaware of his own physical pain, knowing only the loss inside him and the suffocating awareness of his own inadequacy to measure up to what

Finbar expected of him, he staggered inside.

Bretherton, Isla, Candace, and Quinn had all come up from the cellar and were more or less under the table, huddled together. As one, they looked up at Charles as he came in.

"What happened?" Isla asked, loosing herself from Bretherton's arm and crawling forward to stand up. "Where's Walker? You look awful! Did you find Walker?"

Charles should have worked out what he was going to say, but his mind was numb with horror. In thinking of Stefano and Finbar, he had almost forgotten Bailey. Now he had to think of a way to be honest but not brutal, and there was no time.

"I'm so sorry, Mrs. Bailey," he said simply. "The volcano has gotten a lot worse. I'm sure you know that already. It has struck very close. Several of the outbuildings are badly damaged."

Bretherton reached out and put his hand on Isla's arm, steadying her. "Are you saying he's dead?" he asked quite calmly, as if he understood already.

"Yes, sir, I'm afraid so," Charles replied, grateful for the man's understanding and lack of hysteria. "I'm sorry to have to tell you."

Candace was standing up, too, staring at him. This was going to be considerably harder. There was nothing good about this, no relief for anyone, and nobody to help Candace except Charles himself. How on earth was he going to measure up to it? He had no choice, none at all. To evade it now would be despicable. He had to take Finbar's place, at least physically, even if he never could emotionally. The pain of not trying would be worse than any despair of failure.

He looked at her frankly, meeting her eyes. "I'm sorry . . ." He found the words desperately hard to say.

"Was it his heart?" she asked.

Should he lie? Heart attacks could be quick. But he would want to tell her the truth later. Finbar deserved that. His courage would be something to strengthen her for the rest of her life. Charles knew that if he lied now, she would never completely trust him, and she needed more from him than his own easy way out.

"No." He watched her face as he said it. He saw the shock, the fear of something worse. Better do it all now.

"Stefano pushed us back against the wall of one of the buildings, and tried to protect us." He should say it all now, then he wouldn't have to again. "One of the lumps of burning lava killed him, and it injured your uncle . . ."

Candace lunged forward as if she wanted to get past him and go outside. "He's not dead! Why did you leave him?" She swung around to Bretherton. "Come and help me!"

Charles caught hold of her with his arms. She struggled for a moment, kicking at him. He held her tighter.

"Candace! Stop . . ."

She tried to hit him and only just missed his face.

"Candace! He didn't die instantly, but he's dead now. He made me promise to look after you. That was what he cared about most: that you would be all right. He was a brave man, a wonderful man, and he loved you dearly."

She stopped struggling, but he could feel the rigid tension in her body.

"He lived long enough to shake

my hand on it. Then he ordered me to leave him and come back here so I could help to get us all out before the volcano really lets fly. Stefano was sure it will."

Gradually she let go and slumped in his arms.

He looked over the top of her head to Bretherton. "We've got to get supplies together and get on our way," he said. "Stefano had most of it ready —"

Quinn interrupted. "Who put you in charge to make decisions for the rest of us?" he demanded. "For God's sake, Mrs. Bailey has just lost her husband, and Miss Finbar her uncle. You can't expect them to . . ."

Isla turned and glared at him.

"Expect us to what? Want to escape from here and live? Don't speak for me, Mr. Quinn. I can speak for myself, and I imagine Candace can as well." She looked at Candace, still standing in Charles's arms, her face buried in his shoulder. "Candace?" she said again, her voice was gentle but clear.

Candace straightened up slowly and turned to face her. She was pale and shivering, but she stepped away from Charles and stood separately. "Yes, of course I can," she answered. "If Uncle Roger died making Charles promise to look after me, then he would expect me to behave properly. He never ran away from anything; neither will I." She blinked several times and the tears slid down her face. She gave a twisted little smile. "Except the volcano, of course. I think we should all run away from that."

"Well said," Bretherton agreed. He looked from her to Charles. "Let's get started. We'll need water mostly, and I suppose a little food. It's midwinter so it will get dark early. We'd better get going as quickly as we can."

Quinn looked very pale. "We don't want to get caught on the side of the mountain in the dark. We could get lost!" He looked at Charles. "Have you got even the faintest idea which way to go?"

"That will depend on where the eruptions are," Charles replied. Really he had no idea, but they needed to believe in him. Panic was one sure way to make everything worse.

"And how the hell do we know what that will be?" Quinn challenged. They all looked at Charles questioningly.

He must find an answer. Stefano had wanted them to leave. In fact he had been adamant about it. Why?

There seemed to be silence outside. The rumbling had stopped.

"It's finished!" Isla said, her face bright with relief. "If that's the end of it we'd be foolish to risk going out and trying to get down the mountain by ourselves. Wouldn't we be better to go back to the cellar and wait there? Lava bombs won't affect us underground. There's plenty of food. We could stay low for days."

"And if it's not finished?" Charles asked her.

Bretherton shifted his weight from one foot to the other. "I think we should listen to Latterly. What did Stefano say? He's the only one who has actually lived here."

"He said we should go down to the sea as quickly as we can," Charles replied. "All we should take is some food and water. And warm clothes, I should think. It gets a lot colder after dark."

"It's only morning!" Isla protested. "How long will it take us? Surely it isn't that far? I can remember coming up in the pony cart, it only took . . . what . . . half an hour?"

"More like an hour," Quinn told her.

"Even so, that was uphill," she pointed out. "If it took us twice as long, that's only two hours." She looked at Charles. "That's hardly until dark."

"It may not be so simple," he tried to explain. "We might not be able to follow the direct route down. Better we take supplies, and don't need them, than don't take them and do."

"I'll carry yours, with pleasure," Bretherton told her. "And I'm sure Latterly will take Candace's. Quinn can carry his own . . . or not, as he chooses."

Quinn stared around at each of them. "I'll go ahead, if you like? See if I can get someone to come back for you with a horse and cart."

Charles suddenly remembered very vividly seeing the wound in Walker-Bailey's neck and the icy realization that he had been murdered. One of them gathered here in the room had killed him. He had never considered it even possible that it had been Stefano or Finbar; it could not have been young Candace; and he knew it was not himself.

On the other hand, Bailey and Quinn clearly loathed each other. Bretherton he did not want to suspect, but he could not help observing that he was fairly obviously in love with Isla, and loathed Bailey for the way he treated her.

Isla was trapped in a marriage she hated, and it had come to a crisis with Bailey's decision to sell the house she loved, perhaps the only reminder of happier days. It was also close to the churchyard in which her family, including her only child, was buried. The house, the garden, must be full of memories for her. The thought of other people living there, changing it, maybe even cutting down her favorite trees, roses, places where her child had played, was a unique kind of pain.

Could she have turned on him finally? It was certainly not impossible.

"Thank you," he replied to Quinn as courteously as he could. "But I think we should all stay together." He tried to make himself smile. "If one of us is hurt, we may need the strength of all of us to help. We stand a far better chance together."

"Stand a chance?" Quinn said incredulously. "For God's sake, man, it's a few miles' journey down the mountain! And a good enough road all the way. Why on earth should we not make it? Stop talking as if it's a route march through enemy territory. If you're so nervous about it, let Bretherton take charge. He's a military man, used to danger and leadership. Bretherton?"

Bretherton hesitated only a moment. "I think we should all play our parts, and I'm perfectly happy to follow Latterly. I agree with him. We need to stay together. And quite honestly, Quinn, I think it is a bit of a route march through enemy territory. That mountain needs to be taken seriously."

"We've only Latterly's word that Stefano said we should go," Quinn pointed out.

"And that's enough for me," Bretherton said immediately. "Regardless, how long do you want to stand here arguing about it? Let's get the food and water and an extra jacket or two, and start on our way. Ten minutes here or there could make a difference."

"The mountain's quiet," Quinn

pointed out. "It hasn't done anything for several minutes. In fact,
all the time we've been arguing
about it."

For a moment Charles thought
Bretherton was going to lose his
temper, but with a considerable effort he reined himself in. Charles
admired him for it, but it was also
an indication of his self-control, his
single-mindedness where Isla was
concerned. He was a man of little
imagination, not much conversation, but he did not lose sight of
what he wanted.

Military rank could be purchased,
and usually was. But Bretherton
seemed to be one of those who had
risen from the ranks on merit.

If you want to stay here, then do,"

Candace said. "I'm going down the mountain while I can."

That seemed to be enough; Charles and Bretherton began to collect the supplies that Stefano had already put aside and added extra clothes to them. With a sigh, Quinn gathered his own. Charles carried food and water for Candace, but she insisted on taking, at the very least, her own coat. They set out less than ten minutes later. And as if to confirm their decision, when they started along the road that led eventually to the sea, the mountain sent up another huge arc of lava. They could see where it landed on one of the slopes on the seaward side and immediately set fire to the bushes farther down.

They all stopped and stared at it. It was beautiful and incredibly destructive, possessing a violence none of them had seen or even imagined before.

"Come on," Charles urged. "It's not getting any better. We must keep going. Candace and I will lead. Quinn, would you bring up the rear, so if anyone falls you'll notice?"

"Of course," Quinn agreed. "You're right. We should keep going with all the speed we can make."

They spread out a little bit. The road was still fairly level and the going was relatively easy. It would get harder when they reached steeper slopes in the descent.

In the background the mountain kept on rumbling, falling silent, then belching smoke and starting again. There seemed to be ash everywhere, like a fine grit. Charles could feel it on his skin, occasionally in his eyes and in his mouth. The smell of sulfur was quite pungent when the wind stirred and blew from the direction of the mountain.

Candace walked close beside Charles. She refused to cry, but he could see the desolation in her face. He ached to be able to do something about it; but whatever he said, it would change nothing. How did people bear it when it was their own child who was so hurt? He had known this girl only two days, and yet he felt her grief more deeply than he would have imagined possible.

Why couldn't he think of anything to say? If he even told her he cared, how could she believe him? He did not dare leave her to walk alone, but maybe she would greatly have preferred it. Was he an intruder she put up with rather than make a fuss, while they were all trying to escape the volcano?

Or perhaps she was hardly even aware of him.

"He was a great man," he said suddenly. "I hardly knew him, and I miss him. I can't imagine how you feel."

She kept her face turned away, so he wouldn't see her tears, but she put her hand out and took his. She kept hold of it, even though it was awkward having to match his pace to hers so they were not walking out of step with each other.

They kept going in silence for more than half a mile. Bretherton and Isla were ahead of them. Charles turned to look behind and check that Quinn was still there, keeping up.

The mountain fell quiet for a while. Was it dying down, all over, and they were running for nothing? Or was it building up to a really major eruption, one that would send a huge lava flow halfway down to the sea?

Suddenly Candace spoke again, quickly, letting go of Charles's hand so she could face him more easily.

"Somebody will be glad Uncle Roger is dead, you know?" she said with anger hardening her voice.

He was startled. "Really? Why?"

"He was owed a lot of money," she replied. "I mean a real lot. Maybe it was more than someone could afford to pay."

"How do you know that?" he asked.

"He was angry," she said. "Anyone who didn't know him wouldn't have seen it. But I did. He never used bad language, he just said 'It doesn't do.' That meant it couldn't be allowed. It was unacceptable. 'Unacceptable' was the worst word to Uncle Roger. It meant you were finished."

"Do you know who it was?" It wouldn't have anything to do with this now, here on Stromboli, but if she wanted to talk, then he was happy to listen. It was better than grieving silently, feeling as if she were alone.

"No. But it was somebody who cheated him, I do know that. He said he didn't know yet how to prove it." She thought for a moment or two. They walked perhaps another twenty yards. The path was twisting and turning more here, and the wind was blowing the smoke their way.

Ahead of him Charles could see that Isla was getting tired. They had gone no more than a mile and a half, much less than halfway. Still, that was good progress, if the mountain stayed quiet.

"I don't think he cared about the money," Candace went on suddenly. "I think it was the dishonesty that annoyed him. It was something to do with Grandmama. Maybe the money was owed to her; and since she died about three years ago, of course the debt would come to Uncle Roger."

"That means it is owed to you now," he said gently. "Your uncle told me you have no other close family."

She stared at him in surprise. "I never thought of that. I suppose it would. I can hardly collect it, though, because I don't even know who it is that owes it, or how much it is."

He should not have been surprised. Finbar would want to protect her as much as possible. Why had he even told her about it at all?

"How did you know about it?" he asked, then instantly realized how insensitive he was. He could so easily sound as if he were criticizing Finbar, who had no chance to defend himself or explain.

"Oh, it was by accident, really," Candace answered. "We were talking about Grandmama, and he got angry. I thought he was cross with me, and he had to explain that it wasn't me, it was someone else. He wouldn't tell me what it was, just that she never knew about it, and he was glad of that."

"But he didn't say why, or what the nature of it was?"

"No." She smiled a little ruefully. "You couldn't make Uncle Roger tell you something if he really didn't want to. He thought Grandmama was marvelous, more completely alive than anyone else he knew. So she was. I'd love to be like her one day."

Charles wanted to change the subject from Finbar. "Tell me about her," he asked. "What would you like to be that was like her?"

"Funny," she said immediately. "I never knew anyone who could make people laugh the way she did. I love to hear real laughter that's not unkind. Mr. Bailey used to laugh, but it was horrid. The sort of laugh you give when someone else makes a fool of themselves."

She was right: Bailey had had no joy in him, not that Charles saw, anyway.

"What else about your grandmother?" he asked.

"She enjoyed things, all kinds of things — old things she'd had for a long time, like music, paintings, places she'd been to lots of times. But she loved new things, too, things she'd never seen before or tasted, new inventions. And she loved clothes. She was very beautiful, my grandmama. At least I think so." She smiled, as if revisiting memories with pleasure. "She loved hats. She used to wear great big ones, the bigger the better. And flowers — I mean in the garden, not on hats. She would walk around the garden and talk to blossoms, tell them they were beautiful."

Eccentric, he thought, and happy.

"I think you could very well grow up to be a lot like her," he said.

"I won't be as beautiful as she was," Candace said with regret. "You can get away with all sorts of outrageous things if you're really beautiful, you know."

"No, I don't know," he said sincerely. "But I think you don't mean beauty as much as charm." He looked at her. "And I think you could grow up to be quite as charming as your grandmother. You are well on the way to it now."

She walked a step or two, carefully watching where she was putting her feet. Then suddenly she
turned and smiled at him. "Do you
think so? I mean . . . really?"

"I have no doubt," he answered.

Half an hour later they stopped
for another rest. Everyone was
weary, but most especially Isla. She
was probably over forty, and very
unused to this type of physical
exercise. And that, of course, was
added upon the loss of her husband
only hours ago, and the still very
real threat of the volcano. It had
remained fairly passive for the last
hour or so, but the air was full of
ash and dust, and every now and
then there were rumbles in the
distance. They had traveled quite a

long way, but in a semicircle, as the incline of the land made the road easier. They were closer to the sea, but still close enough to the caldera that the danger was real.

They each took a small portion of food, but thirst affected them far more than hunger.

"That's enough!" Bretherton said sharply, when they were all upending bottles to quench their thirst.

Quinn glared at him. "It's only water. You're not in the army now. For God's sake, man, you can't give orders to everyone."

"And where are you going to get more water, when it's finished?" Bretherton inquired.

"From the village well, like anyone else," Quinn replied.

"When we get there," Isla said unhappily. "It's still an awfully long way. I feel as if I've been walking for hours. I know I haven't, but it feels like it, and it won't get a lot easier."

"Have a little more?" Bretherton offered her his water.

She stared at it, then reached out her hand to accept.

Candace turned to Charles and looked at him in amazement. He could see her intense disapproval. There were offers one did not accept. Her expression was momentarily exactly like Finbar's.

Isla smiled and pulled her arm back. "Later, maybe," she said graciously. "I really don't need it now. But thank you."

Candace met Charles's eyes again and her expression again spoke her entire opinion.

Charles hid a smile.

Bretherton kept looking toward the mountain, still spewing smoke and ash. "I think we shouldn't stop for too long," he said, putting away the water.

"The women need a little longer," Quinn argued. His face was flushed and grimed over with ash. Charles thought he looked frightened — as well he should. They were still in danger. He was glad Quinn had not said so aloud. The last thing they needed now was for Isla to give in to her distress. She may not have loved her husband but she would still find life as a widow very different from the comfort she was used to. All things considered, she was keeping control of herself very well.

"Do you actually know anything about volcanoes?" Quinn said suddenly, looking across at Bretherton. "Anything more than the rest of us, that is?" His tone of voice was challenging and abrasive.

"No." Bretherton stared levelly at him. "Do you?"

Quinn looked slightly taken aback. Clearly he had been expecting defense, not attack — or perhaps a plea for unity in a time of such danger, and with three tragedies already behind them.

"Only accounts of Vesuvius," Quinn replied. "Destroyed everything in sight for miles. Took two whole cities, buried them in ash and fire —"

"Very helpful," Charles cut across anything further he might have been going to say. "Vesuvius is nothing like Stromboli. It was dormant for as long as anyone could recall, quietly building up an immense pressure. Stromboli spits and grumbles all the time. It won't be anything like Vesuvius." He was angry with Quinn for making the comparison.

"Really?" Quinn remarked. "You seemed in the devil of a hurry to get us all out of there and begin the route march to the sea. God knows how far it is, or if it is even remotely necessary."

"God does know everything,"

Candace said, looking across at Quinn critically. "So it's true He would have to know this." She turned her face to Isla, then Bretherton. "Has He told anyone?"

Charles didn't know whether to laugh or say something stern to her. But he would sound so horribly pompous if he scolded her.

"I notice you don't look at me," he said to her, his eyes light with humor.

She kept her face serious, with some effort. "I'm sorry, Charles. I rather thought that if He had told you, then you would have told me."

This time he could not help the smile. "Probably I would have." He stood up slowly. His legs ached and his feet were sore. He imagined everyone else felt the same.

Isla stood up stiffly also, and Quinn got to his feet last. "I suppose we'd better move on," he said with resignation. He heaved his pack up on his shoulders again.

As they began to walk, Isla approached Charles. Candace obligingly took a few steps forward to walk next to Colonel Bretherton, instinctively knowing she wasn't wanted at the moment. When she was out of earshot, Isla turned to Charles. "Was Walker alone when he died?" she said softly. "Was it quick? Do you think he knew what happened to him?"

Charles had a sudden hideously vivid memory of Finbar kneeling on the ground beside the body, then bending so low he could see Bailey's neck, and the jagged stab wound in it. He would have known he had been attacked, perhaps even known that he would die. Had he seen who had done it? Did he know why? Had his last minutes been spent in terror?

"I'm sorry, Mrs. Bailey, but I would only be guessing. It seems quite possible he didn't know much."

She glanced at him sharply, and then nodded and moved ahead of him, as if wanting to be alone for a moment.

Why could he not have simply lied and said it was instantaneous — that he would have known nothing, felt nothing?

Or would she then know he was lying, and wonder how much he guessed? She could have delivered the blow that killed Bailey, he reminded himself. After years of bullying, if they had been fighting, her husband would have expected her to yield, as she always did. She could have taken him completely by surprise.

But had she the strength to move him? How far could a sturdy woman, driven to desperation, drag a dead man?

Or had Bretherton helped her?

He did not believe Bretherton would have killed Bailey himself, unless it had been an open battle. It would hardly have become a contest. The colonel was four inches taller and the best part of seventy pounds heavier, not to mention trained as a soldier.

But if he came upon Isla when they were quarreling, and he thought Bailey was harming her . . . No, that seemed unlikely. Bretherton was a little unimaginative, predictable in both what he did and what he said. But he would not slit a man's throat. His own pride would not let him do anything in his estimation so cowardly.

But if Isla had already killed her husband, would Bretherton cover up for her?

Charles had only to look at him now, standing close to her, carrying her water, prepared to give her his own. That question answered itself. And Bretherton would believe whatever she told him.

Was she using him? Would he take the blame for her?

As Isla caught up to Bretherton, Candace fell back to walk next to Charles, and Quinn remained a few yards behind.

"You didn't tell her the truth, did you?" Candace said quietly, keeping step with Charles.

"What makes you think that?" he asked her.

She smiled, biting her lip a little. "People who answer a question with another question are usually being evasive about something."

"But you spoke first," he pointed out. He shortened his pace a little so she could keep step with him more comfortably.

"Did he die horribly?" she asked.

"No, I should think he might have been frightened, because he knew he was dying, but it may not have hurt. It would be a lot better if you didn't talk about it. There's nothing I can tell Isla that will help."

"Do you think she's glad?" she asked after a few paces in silence. "I think I might be, if I'd married someone like that."

"I won't let that happen to you," he said firmly. Then he realized how ridiculous he sounded, as if he had any right to decide anything for her.

"Good," she said frankly. "Her father should have stopped her. I wouldn't like someone like Mr. Quinn either, even though he's supposed to have lots of money. There's no amount of money worth spending your life in misery for."

"I shall keep it in mind," Charles said dryly.

"Do you think Colonel Bretherton killed Mr. Bailey?" she asked suddenly. "He'd be strong enough."

He caught her by the arm and swung her to a sudden stop, facing him. "Candace! Listen to me —"

"I know." She tried to get away from him, but he was far stronger and heavier than she, and she saw he was frightened for her. "It's very unbecoming to speak ill of the dead. But Mr. Bailey was a beast! And I shouldn't even have an opinion at all about Mrs. Bailey and Colonel Bretherton. But they're so obvious!"

"I wasn't going to say that at all!" he protested.

She opened her eyes wide. "Weren't you?" There was disbelief in her eyes.

"No, I wasn't." He spoke quietly and urgently. "I was going to say that Mr. Bailey was very definitely murdered, with a knife to his neck, in the artery, then his body was moved and put where it looked as if a beam had fallen on him. Your uncle Roger saw it first, and showed me."

"Oh! Oh dear . . ."

"Yes, oh dear, indeed. That means that one of us killed him. It certainly wasn't your uncle or Stefano. I didn't, and I'm assuming you didn't. That leaves Quinn, Colonel Bretherton, or Mrs. Bailey. Bretherton and Mrs. Bailey have ample reason to, but though they seemed to dislike each other, I can't think of any real reason why Quinn would have."

"Oh . . ." Candace said again. Now all the amusement had vanished from her face and there was fear in her eyes.

"So you will stay with me all the time, do you understand? If . . . if you need some privacy, I will stand with my back to you, but you will not wander off alone. Is that clear? Not for any reason. You must promise me, as you would have promised your uncle."

She let out her breath slowly, her eyes dark with a new and terrible understanding.

"You couldn't be wrong, could you? About Mr. Bailey?"

"I don't think so, but would your uncle be wrong?"

She shook her head slowly. "No . . ." Her voice was barely audible. "It's not turning out to be a very nice holiday, is it?"

He wanted to put his arm around her and hold her close, like the lost and bereaved child she was, but he was not sure enough of himself to do it.

"Come on," he said gently. Then he raised his voice slightly so the others could hear him clearly.

"We've still got a long way to go, and it's getting darker because of all that ash in the sky." He glanced toward the ever-rising shadow feeling worried.

"It only looks dark," Quinn said irritably. "It isn't really."

Perhaps it was because there was so much else that hurt appallingly — Stefano's death, Finbar's death; the fact that one of them here was guilty of murdering Walker-Bailey; or that suddenly and without even intending to, he had become responsible for a beautiful, bright, and intensely vulnerable child — but Charles started to laugh.

Candace must have seen the absurdity of what Quinn had said, and she laughed as well.

Bretherton looked puzzled. He was a very literal man.

Isla really smiled, for the first time since Walker-Bailey's death. "What is the difference between looking dark and being dark?" she said to Quinn.

He turned to her. "If the clouds blew away, and there's a considerable wind up there, it will still be daylight," he said with exaggerated patience. "For heaven's sake, don't you lose your head as well."

"If the dust blew away, the volcano would send up more," Candace told him. "Stefano told me it's been going on and off for three thousand years. What makes you think it will stop this evening?"

"For pity's sake, girl, it usually

erupts only now and then. To any effect, only two or three times a year. You can go and stand on the rim of the crater and look at it!"

"I know," she retorted. "I've been there! You're the one who wouldn't climb up."

"I have better things to do than climb a steep, totally arid hill to look at an ash tip full of bonfires," Quinn told her.

"Like write another book, maybe?" she suggested. "Mr. Walker-Bailey didn't think you could. But if you wrote another one like *Fire* then we'd all love you for it. I don't know how you could have written it. Lucy was wonderful, full of adventure and dreams. She could see the funny side of anything, and she was brave and kind! My grandmama was like that, you know, and everyone loved her. Uncle Roger loved her." She drew in a breath that was more like a sob, then turned and strode away into the gloom of flying dust and ash.

Quinn sat down with a look of horror on his face, almost as if he had been physically assaulted. After a moment he started very slowly to get to his feet.

It was Isla who spoke to him.

"Don't!" she said very clearly. "She's only fourteen, and she's just lost the only relative she had left. Her grandmother died only two or three years ago, and she misses her terribly. She's got to grieve. Let her find solace wherever she can. Personally I'm very grateful that Mr. Latterly seems to be taking such care of her." She looked across at Charles and smiled.

For the first time Charles saw a warmth in her, a gentleness that made him understand why Bretherton was so drawn to her. Perhaps she had been crushed by Walker-Bailey for so long she had almost had the heart killed inside her. If she had lashed out at him, had she been fighting for her own survival? Did he even want to know that, if it were true?

Quinn looked at Isla, then at Charles. "Well, if you don't want us to go after her, then you'd better go yourself," he said abruptly.

"As you point out so vividly, we haven't time to waste looking for someone who's wandered off and gotten lost!"

Quinn was right, and Charles did not bother to answer him. He turned and walked briskly in the direction Candace had disappeared.

He found her fifty yards away, sitting on the ground with her head in her hands, weeping.

He sat down beside her and put his arm around her very gently, but holding her close to him, her head on his shoulder. He did it without giving it a moment's thought. Only afterward did he wonder whether he should have.

He let her cry. Damn the rest of

them and their impatience. Damn the volcano.

Gradually she stopped sobbing and then after a moment or two longer, pulled away from him, sniffing hard. He had one pocket handkerchief, crumpled but clean enough. He gave it to her.

She took it, wiped her eyes, then blew her nose.

"I'm sorry," she said miserably. "I miss Grandmama terribly. It . . . it really hurts. Now there's nobody alive who even knew her, because Uncle Roger's gone, too. That's why I like Quinn's book so much. Lucy in *Fire* is so like Grandmama was. She was full of stories, too, about going to all sorts of places. She used to walk along the bank of the Seine in Paris, first thing in the morning when the whole city was shining clean. She would describe the smell of fresh coffee and those pastries that are warm and so flaky they fall to pieces in your fingers. Or hot chocolate so thick you could practically stand your spoon in it."

She sniffed again. "Or seeing Sorrento by moonlight, while someone played the violin so marvelously it almost tore your soul apart, and you feel as if you simply had to live forever."

He knew they should go back and join the others, before they lost any sense of which direction they had come. But she needed a few moments more.

"She went to Isfahan once, in Persia. She saw a camel caravan passing in the night. They don't walk like horses, you know? They sort of lurch, without making any sound at all; there was no noise except the slightest wind in the palm trees and the sound of their bells. And so many stars the sky was pale with them, so you could see the silhouettes of the animals quite clearly. How can someone who saw all that and loved it so much just be dead?"

"Are you talking about Lucy in *Fire,* or your grandmother? Because as long as there's anyone who can read, Lucy is never dead." It sounded odd, even trite, but he meant it.

She sighed and leaned her head on his shoulder again. "I mean both. I think I meant Grandmama, then I remember passages from Mr. Quinn's book, and I got them muddled."

An extraordinary thought occurred to him, so powerful and so close in the reality of the dust and the gathering darkness that he barely heard the volcano roar again with a stronger and more violent sound.

"Candace!"

She heard the tone in his voice and pulled away to look at him, as much as she could in the fresh smoking dust and the tiny, abrasive sting of ash.

"What? It's the volcano getting worse, isn't it?"

"No! Well — yes, but something

else. Candace, did your grand-mother keep a diary? I don't mean the formal sort, for putting down dates not to forget. I mean a journal of her thoughts. Did she?"

"Yes, she did. Why?"

The volcano gave another roar, this time sharper.

Charles stood up and pulled her up beside him, still holding her by the shoulders.

"Are you sure? Would she have put all these things in it?"

"Why?" She pulled away a little.

He realized he was gripping her too hard, and eased his hold, but he did not let go of her. "Did she?"

"Yes! She said it kept it all fresh for her, so she could have it again in her mind. Why are you asking?"

Then she froze. He felt all the muscles tighten in her arm, her body.

Now he had to tell her. Maybe she already knew.

"Could Quinn have got hold of it?" he asked.

"Yes . . . he could've. He did know Grandmama before she died. He had heard some of her stories." She almost whispered the words.

"She died before it was published?" he persisted.

"Yes. Almost a year before, or a little more. You mean he stole it, and said it was his? That's why it's so wonderful! Then . . . then all the money he got for it should have been Grandmama's!"

"And after her death, Finbar's,"

Charles added. "Yes, I think so."

Candace shut her eyes tight and clenched her whole body.

"Did Quinn murder Uncle Roger?"

"No," he said with absolute certainty. "He was struck by one of the lava bombs. They were falling all round us. Just very small ones, but red-hot, and with great impact. It wasn't anything human, it was definitely the volcano."

She opened her eyes and stared at him. "What are we going to do?"

He was prevented from answering by a crack so loud it hurt their ears, almost like a physical blow. This time the lava shot high into the air, illuminating the rolling clouds now well to the east of the crater. The heart of it was boiling, pale yellow, and the red glare was thousands of feet up like a rain of fire.

Neither of them spoke, but Candace's hand was so tight in Charles's that at any other time he would have let out a cry at the pain of it. Now he clung on to her just as hard.

After a moment he was able to breathe, and speak.

"We go down the mountain to the sea as fast as we can without falling. But first we see which way the lava's flowing. We can't get past it."

She nodded, never taking her eyes from the rivers of fire that were creeping their way, like the slow blood of the earth, down the invisible ruts and crevices of the mountainside, old gullies, and new crevices.

"It's going to come this way, isn't it?" She said it as a fact neither of them could deny, looking at the scarlet lines like veins, spreading out high on the side of the core.

"Yes," he agreed. "Come on. We need to move."

"What about the others?" she asked, clinging on to him.

"They may have gone ahead," he answered, picking his way through loose-lying scree and rubble.

"Mr. Quinn would, but Colonel Bretherton wouldn't leave us behind," Candace stated.

"No, of course he wouldn't," Charles agreed.

A moment later they heard

Bretherton shouting, "Latterly! Where are you? Are you all right?"

"Yes!" Charles shouted back, even though the voice sounded close. The distant roar and crackle of the volcano made hearing difficult. Should he tell Bretherton about Quinn? He might be risking Bretherton's life, or Isla's, if he didn't.

He caught up with Bretherton, and as the other man turned to go, he caught him by the shoulder, hard enough to throw him off balance. Bretherton faced him angrily, then saw his expression and bit back the words that were on his tongue.

"Walker-Bailey was murdered," Charles said more loudly than he wished to, but the volcano would have drowned out any softer sound. "It looked at a glance as if the beam had fallen on him, but if you got down on the floor and kneeled beside him, looked at the side of the neck, there was a deep stab wound in it. There wasn't much blood on the floor, but drag marks where he had been moved. I couldn't see blood in the dust, and the lava bombs kept landing so we couldn't stay long. But it was clear what had happened."

Bretherton looked shaken, but he kept his composure. "I suppose you have no idea who did it?"

"None until just now. That's why I didn't tell anyone . . ."

"But you do now. Who, for God's

sake?" Much of Bretherton's face was covered with ash and dust, but even in the gloom, the red light showed his shock and perhaps a thin thread of fear as well. He must have been aware of Isla's misery, perhaps recently increased to despair.

"Quinn," Charles answered.

The volcano shot out a tremendous gout of flame and incandescent burning rock. A new flow of lava started down the mountain, creating another river.

"I believe that *Fire* was stolen entirely from Finbar's sister-in-law's journal. The royalties belonged to Finbar, never mind the literary value, which belonged to her. I think Bailey found out, and could have been blackmailing him, or might simply have threatened to make it public."

"Yes," Bretherton said, although his words were now inaudible. He added something more, and then abandoned the attempt and with a beckoning wave of his arm, he led the way back to where Quinn and Isla were waiting.

Quinn glared at Candace, who moved even closer to Charles, then turned and started off down what was distinguishable of the road.

They moved downward slowly. The eruption continued, and as the sky became darker the rivers of fire were easily discernible, scarlet veins creeping ever downward.

It was impossible to speak to any

purpose because the roar was incessant as the lava set fire to bushes, molten rock landed out of the air, crashing on hard surfaces or falling with heavy pummeling sounds on the dust and shale.

The smell of burning was added to by the stench of sulfur. Charles had no time to gaze at the fearful beauty of the destruction, the fire lighting up the sky, the forks of lightning around the crater.

Candace stayed beside him every step. She must have been exhausted, but he hardly ever had to hesitate for her. His own legs were aching, his nose and throat stung with the heat of the ash in the air, and his clothes stuck to his body, in spite of the fact that it was midwinter. He could no longer tell if they were on the right route.

They had to stop more frequently to get their breath. The food was finished, and soon the water would be also. Charles pretended to drink out of his water bottle, then he gave it to Candace. "Drink it," he told her with a smile. "I can't carry you . . . believe me." No one else spoke about it, but they recognized there was no choice but to press on. Surely they could not be far from the sea, and since they were still on something like a road, they would eventually come to a village.

What was Charles going to do about Quinn? He had no idea if there was anything left of Stefano's house, or if the bodies of Bailey,

Finbar, and Stefano himself were buried under rubble or burned by the lava.

With a sick understanding, as if the ground under his feet were shifting and trembling, he realized that no one else knew what had happened. There was nothing he could prove, except that investigation into Candace's grandmother's life might show that she was the real Lucy! But surely, if he had any sense, Quinn would have destroyed the actual diary. If he hadn't before, he would do so as soon as he got back to England.

Everything Charles thought he was standing on, the whole edifice of the truth, could crumble under the slightest test of proof.

"Charles!" Candace's voice, pitched with fear, cut across his thoughts.

He clasped hold of her and pulled her closer to him as the ground beneath seemed to turn into liquid and suddenly he was holding her upright. He staggered backward, still clinging on to her. He slipped and fell hard on his back, she on top of him.

The edge of the path where they had stood had disappeared. More ground was folding in on itself, faster than he could have run.

The sky lit up with gouts of flame and for long, breathless seconds the horizon was red. Then, just as suddenly, it darkened again and the mountain no longer roared.

"Bretherton!" Charles climbed slowly to his feet, half lifting Candace as he did so. "Bretherton!"

"Here!" Bretherton called back a little shakily. "Isla's here. Quinn! Quinn! Are you all right?"

There was no answer.

Then the blow landed out of nowhere. It was so hard Charles dropped to his knees. Without the glare in the sky he had no idea what had hit him. Pain shot through his shoulder and his left arm felt paralyzed, but it did not burn.

Then it was on top of him, drawing him forward.

Quinn. He had waited for the moment when the quake had taken everyone's attention and neither Charles nor Bretherton was on guard. He was powerful, fighting for his life. There must be proof after all. Now Charles was going to die, another victim of the volcano, and there would be no one to look after Candace.

He must survive!

With an intense effort, pain almost making him sick, he got to his knees and then fell forward again as Quinn lunged at him. Where the hell was Bretherton?

He got one blow back, but it seemed to have no effect. Quinn was bending over him, breathing heavily.

Charles aimed a kick, but it landed harmlessly.

Quinn put out both his hands, reaching for Charles's throat.

Then Charles was suffocated by a large soft weight landing on him with great force. He had not cried out. Probably Bretherton would not even know!

Then the weight eased and rolled off him. He tried to get up, but his chest ached and he couldn't breathe. He rolled over onto his side and saw Quinn a few yards away. His head was streaming blood but he was getting to his feet again, lurching to gain his balance. He was coming back, fists clenched.

He staggered as the ground under him slipped away, turning into soft, shivering rubble.

Charles watched in horror as Quinn lost his balance and stepped backward. The whole earth seemed to be giving way, twisting and smoking. Quinn was up to his knees in it. Now he was screaming, flailing his arms, going backward.

The crater was belching fire again as the ground caved in and took Quinn with it, burying him in its fall.

Charles still could not draw his breath. Bretherton was beside him, a hand on his arm, gently.

"Latterly! Latterly, are you all right? Breathe, man!" Without waiting he hauled Charles up and onto his feet, swaying uncertainly.

Charles took a shuddering breath. He tried to speak, but no words would come. He could hardly fill his lungs. Bretherton had found him after all.

Then Candace was there, tears running down the ash on her face. "Charles! You've got to breathe. You've got to be all right! Please . . ." She was close beside him, his empty water bottle in her hand. She was holding it by the neck like a cricket bat.

He started to laugh, jerkily, a silly gurgling sort of sound, but one of pure joy. He drew in a great breath at last.

"We've got to keep going," Bretherton warned him. "The lava's still moving. We're on a sort of cart track and I think it's coming this way. We've no time to waste."

As if to confirm what he had said, the ground shook again and they

271

were aware of the roar of fire higher up, and the wind carried a wall of heat.

"We'd better go as quickly as we can." Bretherton waved. "Do you need a hand?"

"No," Charles said quickly. "Nothing's broken. I'll be fine." He moved his weight gingerly. His body ached, but it was only pain, not damage. "Come on! We should go that way." He pointed with his right arm. "Climb up a bit, out of the channel the lava will take."

No one mentioned that the lava would bury Quinn, if it came that way. Charles hesitated once, wondering if they should try to move him.

"No!" Bretherton told him decisively. "It would take ten minutes to get him up that slope, if we could. And I don't think we have ten minutes to get out of the way ourselves."

As if to validate his words, the mountain hurled more fire into the air, and more thick streams of lava boiled up out of a new vent, closer to them.

They moved quickly, all four together, Bretherton helping Isla, Charles and Candace helping each other.

They moved in near silence.

Charles thought about Quinn. Had the proof of his plagiarism been with Bailey? Could he have gotten the diary somehow? It was of far more use to him to keep it and blackmail Quinn than it would be to hand it over to anyone.

But Quinn could not pay out forever. With Bailey dead, Quinn might have been able to retrieve it, or at least see that it was destroyed. Perhaps Isla would have been next? That was a sickening thought.

But he did not need to fear it. It would not happen.

And Candace could grow up one day and be like her grandmother, passionately alive.

It was another two full hours before at last they staggered into one of the little fishing villages right near the water's edge. The mountain was a beacon in the distance, still sending scarlet and orange and gold fire up into the night.

Strangers came up to them and asked them, in Italian, if they were all right. They were offered cakes and wine. Perhaps in the light of hundreds of candles they looked a lot better than they would by day.

Then bells started to ring, and like a shaft of light out of darkness, Charles knew what day it was. This was Christmas, the stroke of midnight, the beginning of a million new, wonderful possibilities. He remembered Stefano's words: "Time of hope, for everyone."

He looked at Candace and she smiled at him, calm and beautiful and full of courage.

"Happy Christmas, Charles," she said.

ABOUT THE AUTHOR

Anne Perry is the bestselling author of twelve earlier holiday novels, as well as the bestselling William Monk series, the bestselling Charlotte and Thomas Pitt series, five World War I novels, and a work of historical fiction, *The Sheen on the Silk.* Anne Perry lives in Scotland and Los Angeles.

anneperry.co.uk
@AnnePerryWriter

The employees of Thorndike Press hope you have enjoyed this Large Print book. All our Thorndike, Wheeler, and Kennebec Large Print titles are designed for easy reading, and all our books are made to last. Other Thorndike Press Large Print books are available at your library, through selected bookstores, or directly from us.

For information about titles, please call:
  (800) 223-1244

or visit our Web site at:
  http://gale.cengage.com/thorndike

To share your comments, please write:
  Publisher
  Thorndike Press
  10 Water St., Suite 310
  Waterville, ME 04901